DANGER IS THE PASSWORD

STORIES OF WARTIME SPIES

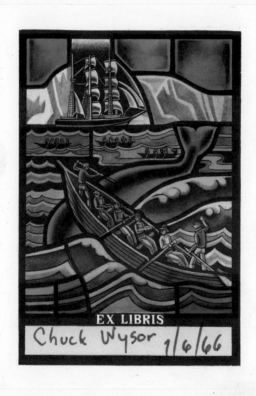

DANGER
IS THE
PASSWORD
STORIES OF WARTIME SPIES
selected by PHYLLIS R. FENNER

illustrated by CHARLES GEER

WILLIAM MORROW & COMPANY   NEW YORK 1965

FOR CONNIE

WITH LOVE AND ADMIRATION
FROM "WAY BACK WHEN"

CONTENTS

LIVING DANGEROUSLY

Spies, counterspies, secret agents, informers, intelligence, espionage, underground, undercover, intrigue. Colorful words that describe a life exciting and dangerous. But there is another side to this picture. Spies, for the most part, are not glamorous people, but ordinary folks like those one meets on the street. Spying is a lonely business, because a spy cannot involve anyone else, and one who is caught **must** suffer alone. He must have a vast knowledge of many little things; he must have patience, discretion, a quick wit, and most of all courage.

Some people become spies for their country, some for the sake of adventure, many for money. Whatever their reasons, they live dangerously. One false move and their time is over.

There have been spies since the earliest days. There were spies in the Bible. As long as man makes war they will exist. All over the world today there are intrepid men and women playing this most dangerous game of all.

P.F.

DANGER IS THE PASSWORD

STORIES OF WARTIME SPIES

NIGHT OPERATION

STUART CLOETE

André Dulac had a gift. It was a gift of God, for he could whistle the tunes of birds, imitating each note very exactly —and are not the birds very near to God? That he could do this was not surprising, though it remained a gift from God, since his father had kept a bird shop in the Rue du Pot d'Etain in the old quarter of Marseilles. To this shop the sailors brought many birds—gray parrots from Dakar, little African finches from Algeria and Morocco. There, too, peasants brought the birds they had trapped—larks, orioles, blackbirds, thrushes, bullfinches. These stood in stacked cages and André helped to take care of them.

But that was in the old days that are gone, and today is today. Let the dead, of both birds and men, who are equally God's creatures, bury their dead; there are many of both;

and many men who kept birds in cages are now themselves
caged. The German soldiers for whom André whistled
thought, in their simple hearts, If he remembers, how does
he sing so sweetly for us? Had they forgotten how the
blinded bullfinch sings or how they teach their own roller
canaries in darkened cages? Was to them, then, the mind of
a boy less than that of a bird, his capacity for recollection
weaker, his passion less urgent?

"Now the thrush, little André," the corporal said.

Then he did the yellowhammer that sits on the thorn in
summer and says, "A little bit of bread and no cheese." As
he whistled, he saw each bird in his mind. André's whistling
brought tears to the eyes of the German corporal of tanks.

"I want food now," André said, "and then I will whistle
again." The birds he imitated whistled for love, pouring out
their passion from a trembling twig or from on high, like the
larks rising and falling as they sang. But he, André, smiling
to himself and at his audience, sang for food and for hate.
How lucky it was that the Germans were so fond of music,
so sentimental about little boys, so home loving.

There was nothing extraordinary in a small boy who took
such an interest in birds wandering about the countryside.
He carried a little box filled with cotton wool for the eggs he
found. It came from the medical officer, and his strength,
because he was strong for his age, from good German rations. The *Herr Doktor* was a great friend. He was an ornithologist and André had once brought him in a clutch of
icterine warbler's eggs—beautiful eggs, pale, pinkish mauve,
penciled with black.

Sometimes André searched near the village, sometimes he
went into the mountains seeking stonechat nests and
wheatears and rock pipits. In the months he had been here
he had learned the country. He knew it much better than
the Germans, for they could not explore as a little boy
could. There were men in the mountains—in the *Maquis*—

bearded, wild-eyed Frenchmen armed with stolen guns. Francs-tireurs, they were called, free shooters and free men, if starving, in an enslaved land. André's hands were in his pockets. His head was bent, for to find a nest in the harsh, uncropped grass of the slopes, one sought the little tunnel through which the parents ran in and out of their nest. Men now were becoming as wise as the mountain birds and, if size was taken into consideration, almost as brave.

There was the cry of a lapwing. André looked around him. He could see no plover flashing its white belly in the sunshine. He sat down and pulled a piece of sausage and a roll from his pocket. Near him, on his left, was a little wood; it reached out toward the more open ground in scrubby growth. Getting up, he moved nearer to a big bush and lay on his back with his head hidden under the branches.

He stared upward at the crisscross of leaves and branches. Against the blue sky, they looked almost black. Nest? There was no nest, no dark, circular patch, no suspicious thickness where the branches met the bole. But one would come, miraculously, while he waited. That was why he had heard a lapwing when there had been none in the sky, for the lapwing only cries on the wing. One had only to wait. There was so much to wait for. The day of reckoning, for instance. The day of traitors, when they would die. The day of revenge. The day of searching, when one would be free to seek *papa* and *maman*. The great day when, having found them, he would help them to open another bird-and-animal shop in Marseilles again. That was what one waited for. What one worked for. Why, in fact, one went bird nesting, collected eggs for German doctors, and whistled bird songs for German privates. A little boy was without much strength; he was unable to join a movement of resistance— or so they said. All he had was guile. All he could do was to set snares, as one did for wild birds. But a thin horsehair noose would hold a large bird, and a little birdlime, made by boiling linseed oil, would catch a multitude if spread correctly. But it was hard to be alone, to be forced continually to match one's wits against those of grown men, to set infantile duplicity against mechanized brutality. Hard, yes, but today everything was hard.

There was a sound behind him. A bearded face was above him. A pair of dark eyes looked into his own. It was Robert. "So you came," he said.

"I came, *camarade*."

"How are things in the village?"

"They are bad. They are going to rout you out. They are very angry. They have a new commander."

"So they are angry. . . . Did you bring any cigarettes?"

André brought a packet out of his pocket. "They encourage me to smoke," he said, "and to drink. It amuses them."

"Pigs!"

"No, *camarade*. They are wise. It is part of their plan to demoralize youth. I am young, and therefore to be demoralized. One sip and I am drunk. I who have drunk wine since I was four, with water, of course, but still wine. Then they talk freely while I reel and fall. That is amusing, *camarade*. I act like a drunken sailor, and have I not watched many drunken sailors? One is not born in Marseilles for nothing."

"Pigs, I say."

"If they were different, I should not know so much."

"You know their plan?"

"Naturally. It is arranged that I am to lead them. I am their favorite collaborationist. 'A little child shall lead them.' *Maman* used to say that."

A great hand patted his shoulder. "Think not of your mother now, my little one. It is too soon. We will find her for you when the time comes."

"They know where you are on the Mont du Bouk, but they are afraid of the straight way up the slope. Their plan is to send some men that way, but the others are to go the back way, which I shall show them. Then in the gorge. . . ."

"In the gorge . . . continue."

"Yes, *camarade*. And it seems to me that the tanks could be blocked in it. It is very narrow, and a little charge of dynamite at either end. . . ." André paused. "Would that be possible? You have dynamite and detonators?"

"Enough for two charges, but if you lead them, you will be in front. There will be danger when the rock falls."

"There will be danger."

The big hand patted him again. "Then it is understood."

"And you will get things ready?" André asked.

"At once."

"There are not many of you—only twenty, I think you said."

"There are two hundred."

"But only twenty fully armed."

"If we catch them, there will be arms for all, and explosives; more are going to be dropped to us by air. I tell you, little comrade, the day approaches."

"You have some eggs for me, Robert?"

"Certainly. A clutch of nightingale's." The guerrilla showed him the eggs, olive green.

This was amusing—that the men of the mountains should find eggs for the German ornithologist. In their wanderings, in their climbings and crawlings, it was inevitable that they should find nests, and they brought what they found to their young collaborator. Yes, it was amusing and terrible.

André transferred the eggs to his own box. "Then that is all."

"That is all, little comrade. But I wish you were not going to be there when the mountains fall."

"It will be a fine sight to see."

In his mind, André heard the crack of the explosion, saw

the mountainside quiver and fall, the rocks rolling and leaping down. Yes, it would be a fine sight. Then another crash at the rear of the column, and the Boches would be trapped. Danger; yes, there would be danger, but he had his plans. It was funny that neither the guerrillas nor the Germans knew what was in his mind. A thousand times he had said, "Let me join you in the hills. Let me be one of you." And they had always said, "You are too young. The life is too hard." But after this he would not be able to go back. They would have to take him, and he, too, would be armed by the dead. Since he would have been responsible for the ambush, they could not grudge him a rifle. He shot well. The Germans had taught him on the range for a joke. And Schultz, the corporal, had taught him the German arms drill, also for a joke. A little sadistic, because at first the rifle had been too heavy for him, but his arms had strengthened, and now often in the officers' mess he did his drill as smartly as a private in the Prussian Guards. Slope arms, order arms, present, goose step—and his arms were like iron. It had taken months, but the moment he had waited for had almost arrived.

He would lie here a little longer and then go back. He looked at the nightingale eggs again. How beautiful they were. They had a smooth, shining texture; they were like miniature pheasants' eggs. How beautiful the song of the nightingale in scented nights of spring.

Birds. Birds were free to fly in God's air, were free to sing; that they sang still, gave one hope. Were free to nest, to live as they had always done. Today there was little singing in the land. The people who had once sung at their work were silent, despairing slaves. The house birds, the canaries, the larks and blackbirds that had hung in their wicker cages outside the cottage doors when the sun was shining, were gone. All France was gone. All that was left was the mountain bands. They were free like the birds, and hunted like birds. He thought of the house birds they had at home. The

canaries, twenty of them, in a great cage in the apartment
over the pet shop. How they had sung, how tame they had
been. His father had been a great tamer of birds and beasts.
Then there had been the final night when there was no more
food for the birds. The canaries had been the last left. *Papa*
had let some of the birds go—the wild ones that could take
care of themselves, trapped goldfinches, siskins, green-
finches. The others they had eaten. And now the canaries.
Maman had made a pie. *Papa* had killed them. Nourishment? What nourishment was there in twenty songs, for that
is what they had eaten, with tears in their eyes.

He had said, "*Papa*, I shall vomit if I eat this pie."

And his father had answered, "Then vomit, little one; this
is no meal. It is a sacrament. It is something to make us remember. It is like the blood of Christ, a sacrament. Our
birds are now part of us, their courage and their songs enclosed within our hearts."

And now, soon, the Germans were going to eat canary pie.
It was indeed odd that there should be twenty armed guerrillas. There had been twenty birds. But now their song had
changed—twenty rifles, held in hard brown hands, spitting
death at the Boches. That, too, was a sacrament; and if he
died, which was possible, from a stray bullet or a shot from a
German pistol, then that also was what was meant to be.
Like the canaries, he, too, would be dead, but he would not
arrive up there alone. With him would come the German
dead, the men he had trapped in the ravine.

He got up slowly. It was time to go back to the barracks,
to the Germans and the collaborationists, among whom he
was numbered. The other children spat on him when they
dared. Once they had set upon him and beaten him, for he
was fat and they were thin. This fatness was the mark of the
beast. He was ashamed of it.

There was a lapwing cry again. And again there was no
lapwing in the sky. He answered it. His friends were wishing

him farewell. In an hour his enemies would welcome him.

Capt. Dr. Otto Seltz was a tall, stooped, prematurely middle-aged young man. The only thing German about him in appearance, had he not been in uniform, was his eyes. They were of that peculiar German blue which is between salt-walter ice and the color of an Alpine gentian, and which have, owing to the way they are set in the skull or to some other quality, a certain stony glitter. André had come to hate the look of these German eyes.

"Ah," the doctor said when he saw him. "You have eggs, *hein?*"

"*Oui, monsieur,*" Andre said. "I have nightingale's eggs."

"That is good, my young friend, that is good. I have them already, but a duplicate set is good to have today, when so much gets broken."

André handed over the box.

"*Wunderschön!* How wonderful are God's creatures!" The doctor paused. "Do you wish to see me blow them?"

"If the doctor pleases."

"Then come." He led the way into his surgery. Here, piled up in cases and unpacked on the shelves, were medicines, bandages and instruments in little glass-enclosed cupboards. The medical wagon would be good loot. Naturally, they would take it along. There was a doctor in the mountains, but he had nothing to work with, only a few bandages that the peasants gave him, made from old torn sheets. The doctor had his egg collection in a tall cabinet. He pulled out a drawer and showed André his nightingale eggs.

"Mine are darker in color."

The doctor compared them. "Yes, indeed they are. These that I have come from the north of France." He picked up a card. "Forêt d'Hardelot, Pas-de-Calais, May, 1941. And now. . . ." He took a little conical drill from a drawer and pierced the egg in his hand in the middle. Then he took a metal blowpipe and, setting his lips to it, put the tip into the hole. As he blew the egg, a mixture of white and yolk flowed out.

"Quite fresh," he said; "not set on at all. Not that it matters. I have blown eggs that were nearly ready to hatch. Only then we have to cut up the young bird inside the egg and remove it piece by piece, and it needs a bigger hole."

"Are they not living, doctor, when you cut them?" André asked.

"Naturally, my young friend."

He took up another egg.

An orderly came in and began to pack some bandages and dressings. "All the usual things?" he asked.

"Yes, the usual, but we are not expecting many casualties tomorrow. They have hardly any arms."

So it was tomorrow, and there was a traitor who had told them how the guerrillas were armed.

"Again, André. March round the table again."

The officers, except for the colonel and the orderly officer, were drunk. It was impossible for the colonel to get drunk. Drinking heavily did not affect him. He seemed immune to all things, to all emotion, a military icicle who neither approved nor disapproved of anything.

"Now the arms drill."

Someone brought in a rifle. It was nothing to slap it around now. If only it had been a loaded submachine gun. From the corner where he stood, André commanded the whole room. In his mind he did it. The cold-eyed colonel with his monocle first, then a quick traverse, at table level, would rip their bemedaled chests to pieces. A traverse and back again. Almost unconsciously, André obeyed the orders a young captain was shouting at him. His mind was centered on his ears. He must hear the talk. It was for tomorrow. Tomorrow night.

If only they had had more dynamite and could have

blown the whole gorge up, instead of just closing the ends. And suppose anything went wrong—with just two charges there was no margin of safety.

A captain gave André a glass of brandy. "Drink to the *Führer*," he said.

André raised his glass. "*Heil* Hitler!" he shouted, and drank it down in a gulp. He held his elbow high in the German fashion.

He could see disgust in the colonel's face. He knew he was thinking, The little traitor. No German boy in his position would do that.

It made one laugh. Now was the time to act drunk. André dropped the rifle with a clatter on the tiled floor. In bending down to pick it up, he reeled and fell. He groped like a drunken sailor trying to find a coin he had dropped in the gutter. His mind was saying, Tomorrow, tomorrow.

The troops were busy—much busier than usual—and had no time for André. They did not know exactly what was happening, but they knew something was in the air. The officers laughed and were gay. "Night operations," they said. Tomorrow had become today—tonight. André had been called into headquarters and had talked to the adjutant and colonel. He was all but a prisoner, confined to barracks, with orders not to leave, and a man had been told off to watch him.

It made one laugh. This fantastic, ingenuous simplicity. For a while at first, one had been dazed at the suddenness of it all. France had fallen. It was inconceivable, but with the shooting of hostages, the rounding up of able-bodied men and women, something had stirred in France—a Gallic subtlety that no Teuton could understand; a something that laughed at efficiency and sabotaged it. That watched and waited. *Mon Dieu,* a simple German soldier could not even blow his nose without the whole world knowing it. A nose blowing could echo from the Alpes-Maritimes to the Pas-de-Calais, from the Bay of Biscay to the Rhine, if it had significance. Of course they would shoot him if he tried to communicate with anyone, but did they really think he had not anticipated these orders and made his plans?

The afternoon passed. The evening came; the light began to fade. The tanks stood out in black and terrible silhouette; the men lounged about in marching equipment, the under-officers shouted and fumed in the state of choler that was normal to them at such times. The coming and going increased, more bombs were issued, extra ammunition. The doctor's camion was being loaded and the stretchers in the ambulance checked over.

The men filed up to the field kitchens for their dinner—meat stew with potatoes, and bread and cheese and coffee. The fragrance of the food filled the air. The smell, which, in a starving country, was palpable, a physical thing, was cut with the knife of the men's laughter and rough talk, the clatter of mess tins and knives. One man played a concertina softly. The word was passed for André.

"Stay with me," the adjutant said. The colonel evidently was not going. After all, a raid against guerrillas was not a colonel's job, but it was a pity. André had hoped he would go. He listened to him giving the captain in charge his final instructions.

"Sound the fall-in."

The bugler raised his bugle.

There was a rush of feet, shouts, orders. The tempo changed with the first note. Order came out of chaos as the lines formed up.

"A simple thing," the colonel said.

Captain Hertzoch smiled at him. "An easy thing, colonel," he said. He wore the Iron Cross, first class. He turned to André. "Now, no fooling, boy."

"Fooling?" André said. "Why would there be fooling,

monsieur? I have contracted to lead you up into the mountains by the gorge, and I keep my word."

"You will go with advance guards, and no nonsense." He pointed to a platoon that stood separated from the rest of the men.

André joined them and they moved off up the road. It was only yesterday that he had come along it from the mountains. Then it had been white, a ribbon extended in the blazing sunshine that led through the half-cultivated fields. It was white still, but a ghostly bluish white, a line where the dark night thinned into a mysterious fissure.

They passed the first crossroads. Yesterday—it seemed a month ago, a year ago. The men were marching at ease, smoking and singing snatches of song. The impression they gave was of a night march, of maneuvers, of an exercise. Only later would the order be given and the column show its true nature with a screen of scouts and flank guards.

The order came to stop smoking and for silence. The mountains loomed dark ahead of them, a black mass against the night sky. The scouts and flankers were out, the attack was taking its initial, preparatory form. The force was pushing out its antennae, like a great insect feeling its way.

The captain in charge came up. "We are near now," he said to André. "This is where we turn off?"

"Yes."

"Then go forward." He turned to the sergeant. "Follow the boy and drop guides as you go."

André turned into the fields. Soon they would come to a wood. There was a small stream along its edge. Then, after passing the willows that bounded it, there was a glade that led to the hills and the gorge. At last they were in it. They waited for the main body to catch up with them.

"Lead on," the captain said.

It was very dark in the gorge, very threatening. André was frightened of the place. He was glad he was not alone; even

Germans were better than nothing. He was a small boy again, and no longer the bold patriot. He looked up at the crags. His friends were up there. They were waiting for the moment to explode their charges. Everything was very silent. Even the tanks moved quietly, as if they, too, mere machines, were awed by the magnitude of the rift through which they were passing. Ahead, André could see more light; in a few minutes they would be out on the other side. Had something gone wrong?

The moon came out, appearing suddenly over the tops of the mountains. And then it happened. There was a flash of light, an explosion, and a great crag detached itself, seemed to hover, and, then, tipping, rolled crashing down. As it came, André leaped toward the mountainside. Up, he must get up. A pistol shot cracked beside him. So they had guessed that he had led them into a trap. But he had made it. He was under a rock in the shadow. In a minute, they would be too busy to think of him. The gorge was filled with dust. More rocks were rolling down. So that was what they were doing. One hit the ledge under which he was lying and jumped onto the troops massed below him. In his mind he saw the guerrillas with iron crowbars, with tree trunks, levering down the rocks that were smashing the Germans below them, mashing them into a bloody pulp. The Germans were firing wildly at nothing. The rocks fell from both sides. There was no escape. There was another big explosion. That would close the other end of the gorge. Now they were truly trapped. Someone was shooting Very lights from above. The whole place was lit up.

André crouched lower, digging into the mold with his hands. The guerrillas began to fire. It was massacre. Screams, shouts, curses. André saw Corporal Schultz lead some men up the hillside. He fell clutching at his throat. A machine gun cut his men down as a scythe cuts grass. So they had obtained a machine gun. All the German officers were dead. And most of the men. It was nearly over. He could hear shouts above him. Robert's men were coming down for the kill.

First came the riflemen, wild, bearded, a few in ragged uniforms, and the grenade throwers. Homemade bombs burst everywhere. Then, following them, came the rest of the band, armed with clubs and sticks. They ran through the riflemen and began to strip the dead of their guns and belts. As they armed themselves they ran along the gorge, shouting and firing at any Germans that still moved. Some swarmed over a tank. André could hear the rattle of hammers. Someone shouted for a bigger wrench. They were dismantling the guns before they set fire to the tanks.

And then suddenly—as suddenly as it had all begun—it ended. There was silence. He heard Robert's voice shouting, "André, André! Where is the little one?"

Now that it was over, the valley was strangely quiet. It had erupted like a volcano, and now was quiet. It was over. The Germans were all dead. It was hard to believe. Very odd they looked, too, in the early morning light—grotesque. There was Corporal Schultz. It was strange to think of his joke about teaching a small French boy the German arms drill. To think of his bellows, his slaps, and his ear pinchings. He had fallen back against the tread of a tank. The other dead lay scattered where they had fallen; stripped of their arms, they looked stupid. But what arms they had had —rifles, pistols, machine guns, submachine guns, bombs!

André looked at the rifle beside him, Corporal Schultz's rifle. That was poetic justice. He had also a fine belt—it had *Gott mit uns* on the buckle brass—and two leather cases for cartridges. There was also a leather holster with a lovely Luger pistol in it. Yes, they all had arms now.

His friend Robert approached him. "So there you are, my little one."

"It is I, Robert, and you see what I have." He pointed at his rifle.

Robert nodded. Then he said, "What puzzles me is what we are going to do with you now. They will suspect if you go back."

"Certainly. Had you not thought of that?"

"To be frank, no. I thought you would be killed either by us or by them."

"I thought that, too, Robert, which is why I hid with such celerity when the battle began. It is fortunate that I am small for my age. I shall be very useful to you."

"To us?"

"Certainly. I am now a franc-tireur. I have proved myself."

"We shall have to think. You will have to be strong to stay with us."

"Strong?" André was on his feet. The rifle was in his hands. "See?" he said. He sloped arms, ordered arms, presented arms, trailed arms, grounded arms, and stood at attention beside his rifle. "You see, my captain."

"I see, and I do not like it."

"Why not?"

"It is German drill."

"Then you, my captain, must teach me the French. One learns what one can."

"Good." Then Robert took his hand. "André, you are one of us now, a fugitive on the mountains of our land. With us, you will starve in the forests and shiver in the hills. With us, you will hunt the enemy like wolves until you are dead or liberation comes. You swear?"

André raised his hands. "I swear," he said. "And together" —he pointed down to the valley—"we will make more canary pie."

"Canary pie?"

"That is what I call it. You prepare a valley, you season it with hidden riflemen, you flavor it with bombs, you decorate it with bottles of flaming gasoline, and when it is filled with Boches, you bake quickly and serve very hot." There were tears in André's eyes. He brushed them out with his knuckles and looked up at the sky. "Behold, Robert, the carrion birds, the crows, the kites, the buzzards, and the eagles, come."

Sure enough, there was an eagle circling on still wings above them. André formed his lips, cupped his hands, and let out an eagle cry, the wildest sound that is heard among the mountains. The eagle swerved and answered.

"Behold our friends, Robert—the scavengers, the wild things, the wolf, the bear, the chamois, the deer, and the eagle. Till it is over, we shall have no others."

Robert raised the cow-horn trumpet that hung from a cord over his shoulder and blew a call.

From all sides, his men came running. All were now armed, all carried equipment, food, ammunition, medicine, blankets, and coats.

"That was well done," he said. "How many are wounded?"

"None, Robert, but we have one man, Etienne Vasseur, killed."

"A pity, but if we have lost one we have gained one— André Dulac, of Marseilles." He put his hand on André's shoulder.

André smiled. His plan had succeeded. He was a guerrilla. He had made his first canary pie. He had a family again, a family of two hundred brothers. And when it was over, they would help him find *maman* and *papa*.

FLOOD ON THE GOODWINS

A. D. DIVINE

Dundas looked out into the fog and blew reflectively on his fingertips. The night was cold, raw with the steady drift of the westerly wind, and the fog poured over the dark bulk of the harbor wall as flood water pours over a breach in the dikes—as evenly, as endlessly, as ominously.

The last grayness was fading out of it now, and within twenty minutes at the outside the night would be down, and the sea as lost as the black earth in a snowdrift. Dundas blew again; not a night for fishing, he decided. Not even for wartime fishing, when food was scarce and prices high.

The complete darkness of the harbor was daunting. No lights showed even on a clear night now, save when the immediate necessities of shipping demanded it. Even to find one's way through the narrow entrance was a matter for caution and skill. Dundas knew that he could do it despite the fog, but whether he could find his way home again was another matter, and this fog might easily be a two-day affair.

It was not as if he were a regular local fisherman—though, heaven knew, even the locals had not gone out this night. Dundas was a "deep sea" man, third mate he had been when the war began, third mate of the *Rosvean*, five thousand tons, flush decked, running regularly like a ferry in the Rio Plata maize trade.

In May of 1917 he had watched the *Rosvean* sink off the Casquets. The incident had made a considerable impression on him, but had in no way affected his nerves. His principal reaction had been largely one of scorn at the poorness of the shooting of the submarine which had put them down.

In that July he went down with his next ship, the *Moresby*, because the torpedo gave them rather less warning than the gun of the previous sinking.

He was picked up after two hours by a destroyer, and her commander commended him on his swimming ability.

That left him with nothing worse than a cold in the head, and at the end of July he signed on again. By this time he had won promotion. He signed on as a second mate.

His new office lasted precisely seven hours, allowing for three hours in dock before the ship sailed. Off Selsey Bill, he being then on the poop supervising the readjustment of a hatch tarpaulin, the ship was struck just for'ard of the engine room by a mine.

The explosion cracked five ribs, dislocated his shoulder, and three parts drowned him.

After he was brought ashore the doctors told him to take it easy for at least a month. By way of taking it easy he went down to Ramsgate, where his uncle had one of the new motor fishing boats. After five days of his aunt's cooking he began to get restless for the sea again. After seven days he was skipper of his uncle's fishing boat, and his uncle was taking a holiday.

It was a small boat, eighteen feet long, open, with the engine under a little dog-kennel cover, and no particular virtues. Tonight the engine had been sulky, diffident over starting, and secretive about its disabilities.

Dundas was inclined to thank it. If the engine had started easily, he would now be out in the very thick of the fog. When he came down to the dock there had been little sign that it would close down on them suddenly an hour later.

He bent down after a moment's rest, and began tinkering with it again. He had found the trouble—dirt in the magneto —and nothing remained now but to put the pieces together again.

The lantern he was working by made a pleasant pool of reddish light in the wide blackness about him. There was little more to do now. He felt curiously alone. Save for the steady lap and splash of the water against the sides of the boat and the stone of the wall, the night was empty of sound. Even the long low chorus of bellows and wails and grunts that normally accompanies a Channel fog was absent.

He finished piecing the engine together, replaced the cover, rolled the strap round the groove and, giving a mighty heave, jerked it into sudden life.

After a moment he throttled down and listened contentedly to the steady purring.

Above him a voice spoke suddenly. It was an educated voice, pleasant, with a faint burr to it. "May I come aboard?" said the unknown.

"Who are you?" said Dundas, startled suddenly out of the calm emptiness that had enclosed him.

"Cutmore's my name," said the unknown. "I'm from the

mine sweeper down the wall. Taking a breather before turning in."

"Mind the weed on the ladder as you come down," said Dundas.

The unknown came slowly down, a pair of long legs coming first into the glow of the lamp, followed gradually by a long body. The unknown wore a heavy overcoat, which appeared to impede somewhat his freedom of action.

"Been having trouble with that?" he said, indicating the engine. "I heard you cursing when I passed a few minutes ago."

"Yes," said Dundas. "She's a problem, she is, but I think I've fixed her."

"Going sweetly now?" said the unknown.

"Yes," said Dundas.

"What can you get out of her?"

"Seven knots or thereabouts," said Dundas.

"And what's her range with full tanks?"

"Eighty miles or so, I suppose," said Dundas. "I've never tried her out, really."

"Tanks full now?" said the stranger.

"Yes—er—" Dundas's tone suddenly changed. "May I ask why you are cross-examining me like this?"

"Forgive me," said the stranger, "but can you keep your mouth shut?"

"I—well, I suppose so; what is it?"

"As a matter of fact," said the stranger, "I'm a member of the naval intelligence service, and it is urgently necessary that I should be landed on the Belgian coast tonight. Almost anywhere along the coast will do, as long as it's clear of the German lines. I've an extraordinarily important job on hand, and it's got to be done in complete secrecy."

Dundas lifted his face away from the glow of the lamp.

"Question of getting close enough in. You know the Belgian coast, I suppose. You know how it shoals? Difficult to get a destroyer close enough in to land me with comfort. The size is against it, too, she might easily be seen by the shore posts. It's essential that I should go by a small boat. As a matter of fact, the sweeper up the wall was to have taken me along, but she's developed engine-room defects. That's why I came along to see if there was any possibility up here. They told me there was a motorboat here. I came along, missed you the first time, and then found you by the noise of your engine."

"You said you heard me the first time," said Dundas. "Heard me swearing."

"Oh, yes," said the stranger. "I heard somebody swearing, but I didn't know it was you. As a matter of fact I went along to another boat up there, and they told me you were farther back."

"And that," said Dundas, feeling in the dark for a screw wrench, "proves you to be a liar, for there was only Terris up the wall, and he called good night to me an hour ago. Your story's a lot of bull. You're coming along with me to the sweeper now."

"I was wondering how long you'd take to see through it," said the stranger coolly. "No, don't move, I've got my foot on the monkey wrench, and I've got you covered with a fairly large calibre revolver. Now listen to me. . . ."

"You swine," said Dundas provocatively.

"No, you don't," said the stranger. "Keep absolutely still, because I shall shoot if you make the slightest movement, and I can hardly miss. I use soft-nosed bullets, too. Listen, I'm going to make you a fair offer. I want to charter this boat; it's absolutely necessary that I should charter it, and if you want it back you'll have to come with me. I've got to get to Bruges before ten o'clock tomorrow, and that means I've got to be on the Belgian coast by dawn. This boat can do it, and this fog makes it possible. If you'll take me there I'll give you sixty pounds, in one-pound notes.

It's all I've got. If you won't do it, I'm going to shoot you now, and make a run for it myself. I can find my way out of this tin-pot basin, and I guess I can find the Belgian coast by myself. It's a fine night for yachting."

The stranger used the same tone as he had used in the early stages of his conversation, but a faint overtone of menace had crept into it. Dundas, thinking as swiftly as the other talked, decided that he meant what he said.

"You wouldn't dare," said he after a moment. "The shot would rouse the whole harbor, and the sentries on the wall would get you long before you could clear the entrance."

"In the fog?" said the stranger scornfully. "I'll take the chance."

"There's a boom across the mouth," said Dundas.

"That's an afterthought," said the stranger equably. "I don't blame you. I'd lie myself if I were in your position, but it isn't any use, you know. Are you going to accept my offer?"

"No," said Dundas. He thought rapidly for a moment. If he could edge back slowly he could perhaps slip the tiller out of its socket and, hitting blindly in the dark, knock the other out of the boat.

The stranger seemed to be able to read his mind. "No, you don't," he said. "If you edge back another inch I'll shoot, and I don't mind telling you that I am a prize winner at revolver shooting."

"Give me a minute to think it over," said Dundas.

"I will if you turn round with your back to me. Do it slowly now. If you move too quickly I'll shoot."

Dundas moved slowly round, shuffling cautiously on the floor boards. Immediately he felt something prod him in the back.

"This bullet will rip your spine clear out," said the stranger softly. "I warn you to make up your mind quickly.

If this fog clears I'm done for, you see, and I'm not taking any risks."

Dundas trod his mind as a squirrel treads its mill, but no help came. It was clear that this man was desperate. Whatever he had done, whatever he wanted to do, it was sufficiently obvious that he was prepared to risk his own life. It was equally obvious that he would not allow the life of any other to obstruct his purpose.

"Come on," said the stranger again; "sixty pounds is sixty pounds to a fisherman, and the season's bad, I know. Heroics won't help you if you're a corpse. Better take my offer and keep your mouth shut about it. Nobody will know, you can say you got lost in the fog, and couldn't get home again— engine broke down or something. Any tale. Come on!"

"Can you give me any help when we get near the Belgian coast?" said Dundas suddenly. "I don't know the marks."

"Good man," said the stranger. "Then you'll do it. No, I shan't be able to help you much. I don't know much about it."

"Oh, well," said Dundas slowly. "Doesn't seem as if I've any choice, and I don't suppose it'll do much harm."

"That's right," said the stranger. "That's splendid. Shall we unloosen the ropes?"

"Er—cast off—er, yes. Just a minute. Let me light the binnacle lamp. It'll be no joke working through in the fog, you know."

"I know," said the other, "but I've been waiting for a fog for a whole week now."

Dundas knelt down and, striking a match, lit the tiny lamp of the boat compass that he carried. The green card shone wanly in its glow. He could feel the muzzle of the stranger's revolver still pressed against his back.

"Sorry," said the other, "but I must safeguard myself till we're out of the harbor anyway."

Fumbling, Dundas cleared the mooring lines, and the boat drifted away from the wall. Immediately she was lost to the world.

Dundas jerked at the starting strap, and the engine came throatily to life. Foam swirled under the stern of the boat, and she surged forward through the unseen water. The fog dragged past them, faintly gold in the light of the lamp.

"We'll have that out," said Dundas after a moment. "The visibility's impossible as it is."

The stranger had squatted himself down next to the engine casing on the starboard side. He stretched out and grasped the lamp, found the wick lever, and turned it out.

They went on into the blackness with only the faint green eye of the binnacle making a sign of life in it all.

After a minute or two Dundas put down the helm gently. "We ought to make the entrance now," he said.

The boat lifted to a little swell in immediate answer, and there was a momentary glance of a high black wall. From its top someone challenged, and Dundas answered, giving his name and the name of the boat.

The next instant they were outside in the live water, pitching a little to the lop that came up from the Downs.

"A-ah," said the stranger relaxing. "And that's that. Now you play me straight, young fellow, and you'll be sixty pounds richer. How soon can we get across. It's about fifty-five miles, I should say—that's seven hours by this boat?"

Dundas shrugged in the darkness. "It's sixty-five miles as the crow flies. We'll have to reckon with the tides though."

"When's high tide?" said the stranger.

"High tide—oh, you mean the flood? Well, I'm not exactly sure," said Dundas slowly. "I'll tell you what I'm going to do. I'll go south and a little east now, and round the heel of the Goodwins, and then stand out with the flood, and get right across. With luck we'll make it by two o'clock."

"That'll suit me," said the stranger, "but why not go straight?"

"Well, you see, this is an underpowered boat," said Dundas slowly. "Don't you know anything about the sea?"

"Nothing," said the other airily. "I was in the cavalry."

"The Uhlans?" said Dundas swiftly.

"Don't ask questions, my little friend. You look after your steering." He settled himself more comfortably. "Remember," he added after a moment, "I still have my revolver in my hand. If you betray me, take me up to one of your patrol ships or anything, we will both die."

Dundas grunted and peered into the binnacle.

For a long hour there was silence. Only the steady mutter of the engine, and the occasional lift and rattle of the screw in the stern glands, broke across the silence of the night. Water noises from the bow and the lap-lap along the sides were somehow merged in the immense silence of the sea.

Only once, far away, they heard a bell buoy, and once the clatter of a ship's bell at anchor. At the end of the hour Dundas spoke again. "We will have cleared the Goodwins now," he said. "I'm going to stand out across the heel of them. Like to see the course we're making?"

"How?" said the other.

"Look at the compass," said Dundas.

"And bring my head in front of you with my back to you?" said the other. "No, no, my little friend. Remember only that I have my revolver and the soft-nosed bullets, and that if I die, you die too. The steering is your business—so long as you remember that."

For another hour they held on in silence, then Dundas heard a slight noise from for'ard. A faint, rasping noise. A moment later it came again, an unmistakable snore.

He nodded grimly to himself.

The snoring went on, grew louder, became more steady, more settled. It was plain that the stranger was fast asleep.

For three hours it went on, varied occasionally by little grunts and slight pauses following a change of position.

Dundas occupied himself steadily with his helm, making tiny alterations of course from time to time, checking them carefully with a great silver watch that he held in the light of the binnacle lamp.

Quarter of an hour before midnight the stranger awoke. Dundas felt the jerk as he straightened up, hurriedly.

"You've been asleep," he said quietly, "for a long time."

The other muttered incoherently for a moment, and then said yes. Presently the implication seemed to strike him. "And you tried nothing, no, no funny business." He paused. "That was good," he said. "You are being sensible, my young friend. Sixty pounds is sixty pounds. *Ach,* I was tired. Three days and three nights without sleep, most of them spent in the fields of the wretched country behind Ramsgate. *Lieber Gott,* I was tired."

"Three days and three nights. That's since Monday, then?"

"Yes," said the other.

"Monday was the day of the big explosion?"

"What of it?" said the other.

"You. . . ."

"Partly," said the other cynically. "Since you are being sensible it does not matter if you know."

"But you are English, aren't you? Your voice. . . ."

"Come, come," said the stranger. "I was at an English school, but you knew from the start. . . ."

"I suppose so," said Dundas grudgingly.

"And how near are we?"

"Not far away," said Dundas. "We should get there a little earlier than I thought, half-past one perhaps."

"Good," said the German.

With long spells of silence and occasional brief conversation they pressed on through the night. Once or twice the fog thinned slightly, so that they could see a boat's length from them over the darkling water. Twice Dundas tried to get the German to tell him why he had to be at Bruges in so painful a hurry, but the other avoided his questions adroitly.

Every now and then he seemed to be listening.

"Strange," he said once. "Strange, we should have heard the sound of the guns by now."

"Nothing strange in fog," said Dundas. "You can hear something that's miles away sometimes, and another time miss a fog gun when you're right on top of it."

The night was getting on now. When Dundas next looked at his watch it was a quarter past one. "We should be very nearly there," he said. "Can you take a sounding?"

"What do I do?" said the other.

"Feel in the locker to your right and see if you can find a fishing line with a lead," said Dundas. "I'll slow down, and you throw it ahead of you, feel when it touches the bottom, and then measure it with your arms outstretched."

The other fumbled for a bit, experimented once, and then after a second cast said "Nine times."

"Call it eight fathoms," said Dundas. "We're closing in on the coast."

Five minutes later he slowed for another cast.

"Six times," said the German.

"Getting there; we're inside the five-fathom line."

Five minutes later they heard the sound of little seas on sand, a soft rustle that was yet loud enough to come over the noise of the engine, and the rustle and rush of their progress. Somewhere in the darkness a sleepy gull called.

"We're there," said Dundas whispering. "Get ready."

The other stood up, wrapping his coat about him. Even as he did so Dundas switched off the engine, and in absolute silence they glided in. Suddenly the boat grated, dragged forward and grated again. The German lurched, steadied himself with a hand on the thwart, and said, *"Lieber Gott."*

"The money," said Dundas.

"But yes," said the German, fumbling in his pocket. "You are sure this is Belgium?"

"By the distance we've run," said Dundas, "and the time, it must be."

"Ha," said the other, "take it!"

Dundas met the other's hand and took a rolled bundle of notes. "Thank you," he said. "Get out over the bows; there'll be a little more than a foot of water, and give me a shove off before you go. I must get afloat again."

The other lumbered over the side, splashed for a moment, and then, bending down, heaved. The boat slid astern, Dundas pushing on the other side with the loom of an oar.

In a moment it floated free, surging back into deepish water. Dundas straightened himself, the starting strap in his hand.

"High tide's at three," he called out loudly.

He heard the other splash through the shallows, and then a scrunch as he reached the dry sand beyond. A voice came clear out of the fog to him: "What's that?"

He heard the feet run on, scrunching over the sand and then stop suddenly. The voice came out to him again: "There's water here. A strip of sand and then. . . ."

"High tide's at three," shouted Dundas again, "but the Goodwins are covered before the flood." He bent down and jerked at the starting strap and the engine woke to life. Sitting down he headed the boat round until her bows pointed a little west of north.

Swiftly he crossed the four-mile circle of water inside the Goodwin sands that he had thrashed round and round so many times during the long night. There was six miles between home and the neck of the South Goodwins, upon which a lone man stood watching the slow, relentless upward movement of the tide.

"Thirty dead in the big explosion," said Dundas softly to himself. "Women, too. Well. . . ." he fingered the roll of notes. "Dirty money's as good as clean to the Red Cross fund. And the Goodwins pay for all."

THE NEWS IN ENGLISH

GRAHAM GREENE

Lord Haw-Haw of Zeesen was off the air.

All over England the new voice was noticed: precise and rather lifeless, it was the voice of a typical English don.

In his first broadcast he referred to himself as a man young enough to sympathize with what he called "the resurgence of youth all over the new Germany," and that was the reason—combined with the pedantic tone—he was at once nicknamed Dr. Funkhole.

It is the tragedy of such men that they are never alone in the world.

Old Mrs. Bishop was knitting by the fire at her house in Crowborough when young Mrs. Bishop tuned in to Zeesen. The sock was khaki; it was as if she had picked up at the point where she had dropped a stitch in 1918. The grim comfortable house stood in one of the long avenues, all spruce and laurel and a coating of snow, which are used to nothing but the footsteps of old retired people. Young Mrs. Bishop never forgot that moment; the wind beating up across Ashdown Forest against the blacked-out window, and her mother-in-law happily knitting, and the sense of everything waiting for this moment. Then the voice came into the room from Zeesen in the middle of a sentence, and old Mrs. Bishop said firmly, "That's David."

Young Mary Bishop made a hopeless protest, "It can't be," but she knew.

"I know my son if you don't know your husband."

It seemed incredible that the man speaking couldn't hear them, that he should just go on, reiterating for the hundredth time the old lies, as if there were nobody anywhere in the world who knew him—a wife or a mother.

Old Mrs. Bishop had stopped knitting. She said, "Is that the man they've been writing about, Dr. Funkhole?"

"It must be."

"It's David."

The voice was extraordinarily convincing; he was going into exact engineering details—David Bishop had been a mathematics don at Oxford. Mary Bishop twisted the wireless off and sat down beside her mother-in-law.

"They'll want to know who it is," Mrs. Bishop said.

"We mustn't tell them," said Mary.

The old fingers had begun again on the khaki sock. She said, "It's our duty." Duty, it seemed to Mary Bishop, was a disease you caught with age: you ceased to feel the tug-tug of personal ties; you gave yourself up to the great tides of patriotism and hate. She said, "They must have made him do it. We don't know what threats. . . ."

"That's neither here nor there."

She gave in weakly to hopeless wishes. "If only he'd got

away in time. I never wanted him to give that lecture
course."

"He always was stubborn," said old Mrs. Bishop.

"He said there wouldn't be a war."

"Give me the telephone."

"But you see what it means," said Mary Bishop. "He may
be tried for treason if we win."

"*When* we win," old Mrs. Bishop said.

The nickname was not altered, even after the interviews
with the two Mrs. Bishops, even after the subacid deroga-
tory little article about David Bishop's previous career. It
was suggested now that he had known all along what was
coming, that he had gone to Germany to evade military
service, leaving his wife and his mother to be bombed.
Mary Bishop fought, almost in vain, with the reporters for
some recognition that he might have been forced—by
threats or even physical violence. The most one paper
would admit was that if threats had been used David
Bishop had taken a very unheroic way out. We praise
heroes as though they are rare, and yet we are always ready
to blame another man for lack of heroism. The name Dr.
Funkhole stuck.

But the worst of it to Mary Bishop was old Mrs. Bishop's
attitude. She turned a knife in the wound every evening at
nine-fifteen. The radio set had to be tuned in to Zeesen, and
there she sat listening to her son's voice and knitting
socks for some unknown soldier on the Maginot Line. To
young Mrs. Bishop none of it made sense—least of all that
flat, pedantic voice with its smooth, well-thought-out, elaborate lies. She was afraid to go out now into Crowborough;
the whispers in the post office, the old faces watching her
covertly in the library. Sometimes she thought almost with
hatred, Why has David done this to me? Why?

Then suddenly she got her answer.

The voice for once broke new ground. It said, "Somewhere back in England my wife may be listening to me. I am a stranger to the rest of you, but she knows that I am not in the habit of lying."

A personal appeal was too much. Mary Bishop had faced her mother-in-law and the reporters; she couldn't face her husband. She began to cry, sitting close beside the radio set like a child beside its doll's house when something has been broken in it which nobody can repair. She heard the voice of her husband speaking as if he were at her elbow from a country which was now as distant and as inaccessible as another planet.

"The fact of the matter is—"

The words came slowly out as if he were emphasizing a point in a lecture, and then he went on to what would concern a wife. The low price of food, the quantity of meat in the shops. He went into great detail, giving figures, picking out odd, irrelevant things—like mandarin oranges and toy zebras—perhaps to give an effect of richness and variety.

Suddenly Mary Bishop sat up with a jerk as if she had been asleep. She said, "Oh, God, where's that pencil?" and upset one of the too many ornaments looking for one. Then she began to write, but in no time at all the voice was saying, "Thank you for having listened to me so attentively," and Zeesen had died out on the air. She said, "Too late."

"What's too late?" said old Mrs. Bishop sharply. "Why did you want a pencil?"

"Just an idea," Mary Bishop said.

She was led next day up and down the cold, unheated corridors of a War Office in which half the rooms were empty, evacuated. Oddly enough, her relationship to David Bishop was of use to her now, if only because it evoked some curiosity and a little pity. But she no longer wanted the pity, and at last she reached the right man.

He listened to her with great politeness. He was not in

uniform. His rather good tweeds made him look as if he had just come up from the country for a day or two, to attend to the war. When she had finished he said, "It's rather a tall story, you know, Mrs. Bishop. Of course it's been a great shock to you—this—well—action of your husband's."

"I'm proud of it."

"Just because in the old days you had this—scheme, you really believe. . . ."

"If he was away from me and he telephoned 'The fact of the matter is,' it always meant, 'This is all lies, but take the initial letters which follow.' Oh, Colonel, if you only knew the number of unhappy week-ends I've saved him from— because, you see, he could always telephone to me, even in front of his host." She said with tears in her voice, "Then I'd send him a telegram."

"Yes. But still—you didn't get anything this time, did you?"

"I was too late. I hadn't a pencil. I only got this. I know it doesn't seem to make sense." She pushed the paper across. SOSPIC. "I know it might easily be coincidence—that it does seem to make a kind of word."

"An odd word."

"Mightn't it be a man's name?"

The officer in tweeds was looking at it, she suddenly realized, with real interest, as if it were a rare kind of pheasant. He said, "Excuse me a moment," and left her. She could hear him telephoning to somebody from another room; the little ting of the bell, silence, and then a low voice she couldn't overhear. Then he returned, and she could tell at once from his face that all was well.

He sat down and fiddled with a fountain pen; he was obviously embarrassed. He started a sentence and stopped it. Then he brought out in an embarrassed gulp, "We'll all have to apologize to your husband."

"It meant something?"

He was obviously making his mind up about something difficult and out of the way; he was not in the habit of confiding in members of the public. But she had ceased to be a member of the public.

"My dear Mrs. Bishop," he said, "I've got to ask a great deal from you."

"Of course. Anything."

He seemed to reach a decision and stopped fiddling. "A neutral ship called the *Pic* was sunk this morning at four A.M., with a loss of two hundred lives. SOS *Pic*. If we'd had your husband's warning, we could have got destroyers to her in time. I've been speaking to the Admiralty."

Mary Bishop said in a tone of fury, "The things they are writing about David. Is there one of them who'd have the courage. . . ."

"That's the worst part of it, Mrs. Bishop. They must go on writing. Nobody must know, except my department and yourself."

"His mother?"

"You mustn't even tell her."

"But can't you make them just leave him alone?"

"This afternoon I shall ask them to intensify their campaign—in order to discourage others. An article on the legal aspect of treason."

"And if I refuse to keep quiet?"

"Your husband's life won't be worth much, will it?"

"So he's just got to go on?"

"Yes. Just go on."

He went on for four weeks. Every night now she tuned in to Zeesen with a new horror—that he would be off the air. The code was a child's code. How could they fail to detect it? But they did fail. Men with complicated minds can be deceived by simplicity. And every night, too, she had to listen to her mother-in-law's indictment; every episode which she thought discreditable out of a child's past was brought out, the tiniest incident. Women in the last war had found a kind of pride in giving their sons; this, too, was a gift on the altar of a warped patriotism. But now young Mrs. Bishop didn't cry; she just held on—it was relief enough to hear his voice.

It wasn't often that he had information to give; the phrase "the fact of the matter is" was a rare one in his talks. Sometimes there were the numbers of the regiments passing through Berlin, or of men on leave—very small details, which might be of value to military intelligence, but to her seemed hardly worth the risk of a life. If this was all he could do, why, why hadn't he allowed them simply to intern him?

At last she could bear it no longer. She visited the War Office again. The man in tweeds was still there, but this time for some reason he was wearing a black tail coat and a black stock as if he had been to a funeral. He must have been to a funeral, and she thought with more fear than ever of her husband.

"He's a brave man, Mrs. Bishop," he said.

"You needn't tell me that," she cried bitterly.

"We shall see that he gets the highest possible decoration. . . ."

"Decoration!"

"What do you want, Mrs. Bishop? He's doing his duty."

"So are other men. But they come home on leave. Sometime. He can't go on forever. Soon they are bound to find out."

"What can we do?"

"You can get him out of there. Hasn't he done enough for you?"

He said gently, "It's beyond our power. How can we communicate with him?"

"Surely you have agents."

"Two lives would be lost. Can't you imagine how they watch him?"

Yes. She could imagine all that clearly. She had spent too many holidays in Germany—as the press had not failed to discover—not to know how men were watched, telephone lines tapped, table companions scrutinized.

He said, "If there was some way we could get a message to him, it *might* be managed. We do owe him that."

Young Mrs. Bishop said quickly before he could change his mind, "Well, the code works both ways. The fact of the matter is! We have news broadcast in German. He might one day listen in."

"Yes. There's a chance."

She became privy to the plan because again they needed her help. They wanted to attract his notice first by some phrase peculiar to her. For years they had spoken German together on their annual holiday. That phrase was to be varied in every broadcast, and elaborately they worked out a series of messages which would convey to him the same instructions—to go to a certain station on the Cologne-Wesel line and contact there a railway worker who had already helped five men and two women to escape from Germany.

Mary Bishop felt she knew the place well, the small country station which probably served only a few dozen houses and a big hotel where people went in the old days for cures. The opportunity was offered him, if he could only take it, by an elaborate account of a railway accident at that point—so many people killed—sabotage—arrests. It was plugged in the news as relentlessly as the Germans repeated the news of false sinkings, and they answered indignantly back that there had been no accident.

It seemed more horrible than ever to Mary Bishop—those nightly broadcasts from Zeesen. The voice was in the room

with her, and yet he couldn't know whether any message
for which he risked his life reached home, and she couldn't
know whether their messages to him just petered out un-
heard or unrecognized.

Old Mrs. Bishop said, "Well, we can do without David
tonight, I should hope." It was a new turn in her bitterness
—now she would simply wipe him off the air. Mary Bishop
protested. She said she must hear—then at least she would
know that he was well.

"It serves him right if he's not well."

"I'm going to listen," Mary Bishop persisted.

"Then I'll go out of the room. I'm tired of his lies."

"You're his mother, aren't you?"

"That's not my fault. I didn't choose—like you did. I tell
you I won't listen to it."

Mary Bishop turned the knob. "Then stop your ears," she
cried in a sudden fury, and heard David's voice coming
over.

"The lies," he was saying, "put over by the British capi-
talist press. There has not even been a railway accident,
let alone any sabotage, at the place so persistently mentioned in the broadcasts from England. Tomorrow I am
leaving myself for the so-called scene of the accident, and
I propose in my broadcast the day after tomorrow to give
you an impartial observer's report, with records of the very
railwaymen who are said to have been shot for sabotage.
Tomorrow, therefore, I shall not be on the air. . . ."

"Oh, thank God, thank God," Mary Bishop said.

The old woman grumbled by the fire. "You haven't
much to thank Him for."

"You don't know how much."

All next day she found herself praying, although she
didn't much believe in prayer. She visualized that station

"on the Rhine not far from Wesel"—and not far either from
the Dutch frontier. There must be some method of getting
across—with the help of that unknown worker—possibly in
a refrigerating van. No idea was too fantastic to be true.
Others had succeeded before him.

All through the day she tried to keep pace with him—he
would have to leave early, and she imagined his cup of
ersatz coffee and the slow wartime train taking him south
and west. She thought of his fear and of his excitement—he
was coming home to her. Ah, when he landed safely, what a
day that would be! The papers then would have to eat their
words—no more Dr. Funkhole and no more of this place,
side by side with his unloving mother.

At midday, she thought, he has arrived; he has his black
disks with him to record the men's voices; he is probably
watched, but he will find his chance—and now he is not
alone. He has someone with him helping him. In one way or
another he will miss his train home. The freight train will
draw in; perhaps a signal will stop it outside the station.
She saw it all so vividly, as the early winter dark came
down, and she blacked the windows out, that she found herself thankful he possessed, as she knew, a white mackintosh.
He would be less visible waiting there in the snow.

Her imagination took wings, and by dinner time she felt
sure that he was already on the way to the frontier. That
night there was no broadcast from Dr. Funkhole, and she
sang as she bathed, and old Mrs. Bishop beat furiously on
her bedroom floor above.

In bed she could almost feel herself vibrating with the
heavy movement of *his* train. She saw the landscape going
by outside—there must be a crack in any van in which he
lay hid, so that he could mark the distances. It was very
much the landscape of Crowborough, spruces powdered
with snow, the wide dreary waste they called a forest, dark
avenues—she fell asleep.

When she woke she was still happy. Perhaps before night she would receive a cable from Holland, but if it didn't come she would not be anxious because so many things in wartime might delay it. It didn't come.

That night she made no attempt to turn on the radio, so old Mrs. Bishop changed her tactics again. "Well," she said, "aren't you going to listen to your husband?"

"He won't be broadcasting." Very soon now she could turn on his mother in triumph and say, "There, I knew it all the time, my husband's a hero."

"That was last night."

"He won't be broadcasting again."

"What do you mean? Turn it on and let me hear."

There was no harm in proving that she knew. She turned it on.

A voice was talking in German—something about an accident and English lies, she didn't bother to listen. She felt too happy. "There," she said, "I told you. It's not David."

And then David spoke.

He said, "You have been listening to the actual voices of the men your English broadcasters have told you were shot by the German police. Perhaps now you will be less inclined to believe the exaggerated stories you hear of life inside Germany today."

"There," old Mrs. Bishop said, "I told you."

And all the world, she thought, will go on telling me now, forever—Dr. Funkhole. He never got those messages. He's there for keeps. David's voice said with curious haste and harshness, "The fact of the matter is—"

He spoke rapidly for about two minutes as if he were afraid they would fade him at any moment, and yet it sounded harmless enough, the old stories about plentiful food and how much you could buy for an English pound, figures. But some of the examples this time, she thought with dread, are surely so fantastic that even the German brain will realize something is wrong. How had he ever dared to show *this* copy to his chiefs?

She could hardly keep pace with her pencil, so rapidly did he speak. The words grouped themselves on her pad: "Five U's refueling *hodie* noon 53.23 by 10.5. News reliable source Wesel so returned. Talk unauthorized. The end."

"This order. Many young wives I feel enjoy giving one"— he hesitated—"one's day's butter in every dozen—" the voice faded, gave out altogether. She saw on her pad: *"To my wife, good-bie d. . . ."*

The end, good-by, the end—the words rang on like funeral bells. She began to cry, sitting as she had done before, close up against the radio set. Old Mrs. Bishop said with a kind of delight, "He ought never to have been born. I never wanted him. The coward!" Now Mary Bishop could stand no more of it.

"Oh," she cried to her mother-in-law across the little overheated, over-furnished Crowborough room, "if only he were a coward, if only he were. But he's a hero, a damned hero, a hero, a hero—" she cried hopelessly on, feeling the room reel round her, and dimly supposing behind all the pain and horror that one day she would have to feel, like other women, pride.

THE BOY WHO CRIED WOLF

RICHARD HARDING DAVIS

Before he finally arrested him, Jimmie Sniffen had seen the man with the golf cap, and the blue eyes that laughed at you three times. Twice, unexpectedly, he had come upon him in a wood road and once on Round Hill where the stranger was pretending to watch the sunset. Jimmie knew people do not climb hills merely to look at sunsets, so he was not deceived. He guessed the man was a German spy seeking gun sites, and secretly vowed to stalk him. From that moment, had the stranger known it, he was as good as dead. For a Boy Scout with badges on his sleeve for stalking and pathfinding, not to boast of others for gardening and cooking, can outwit any spy. Even had General Baden-Powell remained in Mafeking and not invented the Boy Scout,

Jimmie Sniffen would have been one. Because by birth he was a boy, and by inheritance a scout. In Westchester County the Sniffens are one of the county families. If it isn't a Sarles, it's a Sniffen; and with Brundages, Platts, and Jays, the Sniffens date back to when the acres of the first Charles Ferris ran from the Boston Post Road to the coach road to Albany, and when the first Gouverneur Morris stood on one of his hills and saw the Indian canoes in the Hudson and in the Sound and rejoiced that all the land between belonged to him.

If you do not believe in heredity, the fact that Jimmie's great-great-grandfather was a scout for General Washington and hunted deer, and even bear, over exactly the same hills where Jimmie hunted weasels will count for nothing. It will not explain why to Jimmie, from Tarrytown to Port Chester, the hills, the roads, the woods, and the cow paths, caves, streams, and springs hidden in the woods were as familiar as his own kitchen garden.

Nor explain why, when you could not see a Pease and El-liman *For Sale* sign nailed to a tree, Jimmie could see in the highest branches a last year's bird's nest with its telltale evidence.

Or why, when he was out alone playing Indians and had sunk his Scout axe into a fallen log and then scalped the log, he felt that once before in those same woods he had trailed that same Indian, and with his own tomahawk split open his skull. Sometimes when he knelt to drink at a secret spring in the forest, the autumn leaves would crackle, and he would raise his eyes fearing to see a panther facing him.

"But there ain't no panthers in Westchester," Jimmie would reassure himself. And in the distance the roar of an automobile climbing a hill with the muffler open would seem to suggest he was right. But still Jimmie remembered once before he had knelt at that same spring, and that when he raised his eyes he had faced a crouching panther.

"Mebbe Dad told me it happened to Grandpop," Jimmie would explain, "or I dreamed it, or, mebbe, I read it in a story book."

The German spy mania attacked Round Hill after the visit to the Boy Scouts of Clevering Gould, the war correspondent. He was spending the weekend with "Squire" Harry Van Vorst, and as young Van Vorst, besides being a justice of the peace and a Master of Beagles and president of the Country Club, was also a local councilman for the Round Hill Scouts, he brought his guest to a campfire meeting to talk to them. In deference to his audience, Gould told them of the Boy Scouts he had seen in Belgium and of the part they were playing in the great war. It was his peroration that made trouble.

"And any day," he assured his audience, "this country may be at war with Germany; and every one of you boys will be expected to do his bit. You can begin now. When the Germans land it will be near New Haven, or New Bedford. They will first capture the munition works at Springfield, Hartford, and Watervliet so as to make sure of their ammunition, and then they will start for New York City. They will follow the New Haven and New York Central railroads, and march straight through this village. I haven't the least doubt," exclaimed the enthusiastic war prophet, "that at this moment German spies are as thick in Westchester as blackberries. They are here to select camp sites and gun positions, to find out which of these hills enfilade the others and to learn to what extent their armies can live on the country. They are counting the cows, the horses, the barns and where fodder is stored; and they are marking down on their maps the wells and streams."

As though at that moment a German spy might be crouching behind the door, Mr. Gould spoke in a whisper. "Keep your eyes open!" he commanded. "Watch every stranger. If he acts suspiciously, get word quick to your sheriff, or to Judge Van Vorst here. Remember the Scouts' motto, 'Be Prepared!' "

That night as the Scouts walked home, behind each wall and hayrick they saw spiked helmets.

Young Van Vorst was extremely annoyed.

"Next time you talk to my Scouts," he declared, "you'll talk on 'Votes for Women.' After what you said tonight every real estate agent who dares open a map will be arrested. We're not trying to drive people away from Westchester, we're trying to sell them building sites."

"You are not!" retorted his friend. "You own half the county now, and you're trying to buy the other half."

"I'm a justice of the peace," explained Van Vorst. "I don't know why I am, except that they wished it on me. All I get out of it is trouble. The Italians make charges against my best friends for speeding, and I have to fine them, and my best friends bring charges against the Italians for poaching. When I fine the Italians they send me Black Hand letters. And now every day I'll be asked to issue a warrant for a German spy who is selecting gun sites. And he will turn out to be a millionaire who is tired of living at the Ritz Carlton and wants to own his own home and his own golf links. And he'll be so hot at being arrested that he'll take his millions to Long Island and try to break into the Piping Rock Club. And it will be your fault!"

The young justice of the peace was right. At least so far as Jimmie Sniffen was concerned, the words of the war prophet had filled one mind with unrest. In the past Jimmie's idea of a holiday had been to spend it scouting in the woods. In this pleasure he was selfish. He did not want companions who talked, and trampled upon the dead leaves so that they frightened the wild animals and gave the Indians warning. Jimmie liked to pretend. He liked to fill the woods with wary and hostile adversaries. It was a game of his own inventing. If he crept to the top of a hill and, on peering over it, surprised a fat woodchuck, he pretended the woodchuck was a bear, weighing two hundred pounds; if, himself unobserved, he could lie and watch, off its guard, a rabbit, squirrel, or, most difficult of all, a crow, it became a deer and that night at supper Jimmie made believe he was eating venison. Sometimes he was a scout of the Continental Army and carried dispatches to General Washington. The rules of that game were that if any man ploughing in the fields, or cutting trees in the woods, or even approaching along the same road, saw Jimmie before Jimmie saw him, Jimmie was taken prisoner, and before sunrise was shot as a spy. He was seldom shot. Or else why on his sleeve was the badge for stalking? But always making believe became monotonous. Even "dry shopping" along the Rue de la Paix, when you pretend you can have anything you see in any window, leaves one just as rich, but unsatisfied. So the advice of the war correspondent to seek out German spies came to Jimmie like a day at the circus, like a week at the Danbury Fair. It was a chance to play in earnest the game in which he most delighted. No longer need he pretend. No longer need he waste his energies in watching, unobserved, a greedy rabbit rob a carrot field. The game now was his fellowman and his enemy; not only his enemy, but the enemy of his country.

In his first effort Jimmie was not entirely successful. The man looked the part perfectly; he wore an auburn beard, disguising spectacles, and he carried a suspicious knapsack. But he turned out to be a professor from the Museum of Natural History, who wanted to dig for Indian arrowheads. And when Jimmie threatened to arrest him, the indignant gentleman arrested Jimmie. Jimmie escaped only by leading the professor to a secret cave of his own, though on someone else's property, where one not only could dig for arrowheads, but find them. The professor was delighted, but for Jimmie it was a great disappointment. The week following Jimmie was again disappointed.

On the bank of the Kensico Reservoir, he came upon a man who was acting in a mysterious and suspicious manner. He was making notes in a book, and his runabout which he had concealed in a wood road was stuffed with blueprints. It did not take Jimmie long to guess his purpose. He was planning to blow up the Kensico Dam, and cut off the water supply of New York City. Seven millions of people without water! Without firing a shot, New York must surrender! At the thought Jimmie shuddered and, at the risk of his life, by clinging to the tail of a motor truck, he followed the runabout into White Plains. But there it developed the mysterious stranger, so far from wishing to destroy the Kensico Dam, was the state engineer who had built it, and, also, a large part of the Panama Canal. Nor in his third effort was Jimmie more successful. From the heights of Pound Ridge he discovered on a hilltop below him a man working alone upon a basin of concrete. The man was a German-American, and already on Jimmie's list of suspects. That for the use of the German artillery he was preparing a concrete bed for a siege gun was only too evident. But closer investigation proved that the concrete was only two inches thick. And the hyphenated one explained that the basin was built over a spring, in the waters of which he planned to erect a fountain and raise goldfish. It was a bitter blow. Jimmie became discouraged. Meeting Judge Van Vorst one day in the road he told him his troubles. The young judge proved unsympathetic. "My advice to you, Jimmie," he said, "is to go slow. Accusing everybody of espionage is a very serious matter. If you call a man a spy, it's sometimes hard for him to disprove it; and the name sticks. So, go slow—very slow. Before you arrest any more people, come to me first for a warrant."

• • •

Besides being a farmer in a small way, Jimmie's father
was a handy man with tools. He had no union card, but, in
laying shingles along a blue check line, few were as expert.
It was August, there was no school, and Jimmie was carrying a dinner pail to where his father was at work on a new
barn. He made a crosscut through the woods, and came
upon the young man in the golf cap. The stranger nodded,
and his eyes, which seemed to be always laughing, smiled
pleasantly. But he was deeply tanned, and, from the waist
up, held himself like a soldier, so, at once, Jimmie mis-
trusted him. Early the next morning Jimmie met him again.
It had not been raining, but the clothes of the young man
were damp. Jimmie guessed that while the dew was still on
the leaves the young man had been forcing his way through
underbrush. The stranger must have remembered Jimmie,
for he laughed and exclaimed:

"Ah, my friend with the dinner pail! It's luck you haven't
got it now, or I'd hold you up. I'm starving!"

Jimmie smiled in sympathy. "It's early to be hungry,"
said Jimmie. "When did you have your breakfast?"

"I didn't." The young man laughed. "I went out to walk
up an appetite, and I lost myself. But I haven't lost my appetite. Which is the shortest way back to Bedford?"

"The first road to your right," said Jimmie.

"Is it far?" asked the stranger anxiously. That he was
very hungry was evident.

"It's a half-hour's walk," said Jimmie.

"If I live that long," corrected the young man, and
stepped out briskly.

Jimmie knew that within a hundred yards a turn in the
road would shut him from sight. So, he gave the stranger
time to walk that distance, and then, diving into the wood
that lined the road, stalked him. From behind a tree he saw
the stranger turn and look back, and seeing no one in the

road behind him, also leave it and plunge into the woods.

He had not turned toward Bedford; he had turned to the left. Like a runner stealing bases, Jimmie slipped from tree to tree. Ahead of him he heard the stranger trampling upon dead twigs, moving rapidly as one who knew his way. At times through the branches Jimmie could see the broad shoulders of the stranger, and again could follow his progress only by the noise of the crackling twigs. When the noises ceased, Jimmie guessed the stranger had reached the wood road, grass grown and moss covered, that led to Middle Patent. So, he ran at right angles until he also reached it, and as now he was close to where it entered the main road, he approached warily. But he was too late. There was a sound like the whir of a rising partridge, and ahead of him from where it had been hidden, a gray touring car leaped into the highway. The stranger was at the wheel. Throwing behind it a cloud of dust, the car raced toward Greenwich. Jimmie had time to note only that it bore a Connecticut State license; that in the wheel ruts the tires printed little V's, like arrowheads.

For a week Jimmie saw nothing of the spy, but for many hot and dusty miles he stalked arrowheads. They lured him north, they lured him south, they were stamped in soft asphalt, in mud, dust, and fresh-spread tarvia. Wherever Jimmie walked, arrowheads ran before. In his sleep as in his copybook, he saw endless chains of V's. But not once could he catch up with the wheels that printed them. A week later, just at sunset as he passed below Round Hill, he saw the stranger on top of it. On the skyline, in silhouette against the sinking sun, he was as conspicuous as a flagstaff. But to approach him was impossible. For acres Round Hill offered no other cover than stubble. It was as bald as a skull. Until the stranger chose to descend, Jimmie must wait. And the stranger was in no haste. The sun sank, and from the west Jimmie saw him turn his face east toward the Sound.

A storm was gathering, drops of rain began to splash and as the sky grew black the figure on the hilltop faded into the darkness. And then, at the very spot where Jimmie had last seen it, there suddenly flared two tiny flashes of fire. Jimmie leaped from cover. It was no longer to be endured. The spy was signalling. The time for caution had passed, now was the time to act. Jimmie raced to the top of the hill, and found it empty. He plunged down it, vaulted a stone wall, forced his way through a tangle of saplings, and held his breath to listen. Just beyond him, over a jumble of rocks, a hidden stream was tripping and tumbling. Joyfully it laughed and gurgled. Jimmie turned hot. It sounded as though from the darkness the spy mocked him. Jimmie shook his fist at the enshrouding darkness. Above the tumult of the coming storm and the tossing treetops, he raised his voice: "You wait!" he shouted. "I'll get you yet! Next time I'll bring a gun."

Next time was the next morning. There had been a hawk hovering over the chicken yard, and Jimmie used that fact to explain his borrowing the family shotgun. He loaded it with buckshot and, in the pocket of his shirt, buttoned his license to "hunt, pursue and kill, to take with traps or other devices."

He remembered that Judge Van Vorst had warned him, before he arrested more spies, to come to him for a warrant. But with an impatient shake of the head Jimmie tossed the recollection from him. After what he had seen he could not possibly be again mistaken. He did not need a warrant. What he had seen was his warrant—plus the shotgun.

As a pathfinder should, he planned to take up the trail where he had lost it, but before he reached Round Hill, he found a warmer trail. Before him, stamped clearly in the road still damp from the rain of the night before, two lines of little arrowheads pointed the way. They were so fresh that at each twist in the road, lest the car should be just beyond him, Jimmie slackened his steps. After half a mile the scent grew hot. The tracks were deeper, the arrowheads more clearly cut, and Jimmie broke into a run. Then the arrowheads swung suddenly to the right and, in a clearing at the edge of a wood, were lost. But the tires had pressed deep into the grass, and just inside the wood, he found the car. It was empty. Jimmie was drawn two ways. Should he seek the spy on the nearest hilltop, or, until the owner returned, wait by the car? Between lying in ambush and action, Jimmie preferred action. But he did not climb the hill nearest the car; he climbed the hill that overlooked that hill.

Flat on the ground, hidden in the goldenrod, he lay motionless. Before him, for fifteen miles away to his right rose the stone steeple, and the red roofs of Greenwich. Directly before him were no signs of habitation, only green forests, green fields, gray stone walls, and, where a road ran uphill, a splash of white that quivered in the heat. The storm of the night before had washed the air. Each leaf stood by itself. Nothing stirred; and in the glare of the August sun every detail of the landscape was as distinct as those in a colored photograph, and as still.

In his excitement the Scout was trembling.

"If he moves," he sighed happily, "I've got him!"

Opposite, across a little valley, was the hill at the base of which he had found the car. The slope toward him was bare, but the top was crowned with a thick wood; and along its crest, as though establishing an ancient boundary, ran a stone wall, moss covered and wrapped in poison ivy. In places, the branches of the trees, reaching out to the sun, overhung the wall and hid it in black shadows. Jimmie divided the hill into sectors. He began at the right, and slowly followed the wall. With his eyes he took it apart, stone by stone. Had a chipmunk raised his head, Jimmie would have seen him. So, when from the stone wall, like the reflection of the sun upon a windowpane, something flashed, Jimmie knew he had found his spy. A pair of binoculars had betrayed him. Jimmie now saw him clearly. He sat on the ground at the top of the hill opposite, in the deep shadow of an oak, his back against the stone wall. With the binoculars to his eyes he had leaned too far forward, and upon the glass the sun had flashed a warning.

Jimmie appreciated that his attack must be made from the rear. Backward, like a crab, he wriggled free of the goldenrod and, hidden by the contour of the hill, raced up the opposite one. When he came to within twenty feet of the oak beneath which he had seen the stranger, he stood erect, and as though avoiding a live wire stepped on tiptoe to the wall. The stranger still sat against it. The binoculars hung from a cord around his neck. Across his knees was spread a map. He was marking it with a pencil, and as he worked he hummed a tune.

Jimmie knelt, and resting the gun on the top of the wall, covered him. "Throw up your hands!" he commanded.

The stranger did not start. Except that he raised his eyes he gave no sign that he had heard. His eyes stared across the little sun-filled valley. They were half-closed as though in study, as though perplexed by some deep and intricate problem. They appeared to see beyond the sun-filled valley some place of greater moment, some place far distant.

Then the eyes smiled, and slowly, as though his neck were stiff—but still smiling—the stranger turned his head. When he saw the boy, his smile was swept away in waves of surprise, amazement, and disbelief. These were followed instantly by an expression of the most acute alarm. "Don't point that thing at me!" shouted the stranger. "Is it loaded?" With his cheek pressed to the stock and his eye squinted down the length of the brown barrel, Jimmie nodded. The stranger flung up his open palms. They accented his expression of amazed incredulity. He seemed to be exclaiming, "Can such things be?"

"Get up!" commanded Jimmie.

With alacrity the stranger arose.

"Walk over there," ordered the Scout. "Walk backward. "Stop! Take off those field glasses and throw them to me." Without removing his eyes from the gun the stranger lifted the binoculars from his neck and tossed them to the stone wall. "See here!" he pleaded. "If you'll only point that damned blunderbuss the other way, you can have the glasses, and my watch, and clothes, and all my money; only don't—"

Jimmie flushed crimson. "You can't bribe me," he growled. At least, he tried to growl, but because his voice was changing, or because he was excited, the growl ended in a high squeak. With mortification, Jimmie flushed a deeper crimson. But the stranger was not amused. At Jimmie's words he seemed rather the more amazed.

"I'm not trying to bribe you," he protested. "If you don't want anything, why are you holding me up?"

"I'm not," returned Jimmie. "I'm arresting you!"

The stranger laughed with relief. Again his eyes smiled. "Oh," he cried, "I see! Have I been trespassing?"

With a glance Jimmie measured the distance between himself and the stranger. Reassured, he lifted one leg after the other over the wall. "If you try to rush me," he warned, "I'll shoot you full of buckshot."

The stranger took a hasty step backward. "Don't worry about that," he exclaimed. "I'll not rush you. Why am I arrested?"

Hugging the shotgun with his left arm, Jimmie stooped and lifted the binoculars. He gave them a swift glance, slung them over his shoulder, and again clutched his weapon. His expression was now stern and menacing. "The name on them," he accused, "is 'Weiss, Berlin.' Is that your name?"

The stranger smiled, but corrected himself, and replied gravely, "That's the name of the firm that makes them."

Jimmie exclaimed in triumph. "Hah!" he cried. "Made in Germany!"

The stranger shook his head. "I don't understand," he said. "Where would a Weiss glass be made?" With polite insistence he repeated, "Would you mind telling me why I am arrested, and who you might happen to be?"

Jimmie did not answer. Again he stooped and picked up the map and, as he did so, for the first time the face of the stranger showed that he was annoyed. Jimmie was not at home with maps. They told him nothing. But the penciled notes on this one made easy reading. At his first glance he saw, "Correct range, 1,800 yards"; "this stream not fordable"; "slope of hill 15 degrees inaccessible for artillery"; "wire entanglements here"; "forage for five squadrons."

Jimmie's eyes flashed. He shoved the map inside his shirt, and with the gun motioned toward the base of the hill. "Keep forty feet ahead of me," he commanded, "and walk to your car." The stranger did not seem to hear him. He spoke with irritation.

"I suppose," he said, "I'll have to explain to you about that map."

"Not to me, you won't," declared his captor. "You're going to drive straight to Judge Van Vorst's, and explain to him!"

The stranger tossed his arms even higher. "Thank God!" he exclaimed.

With his prisoner Jimmie encountered no further trouble. He made a willing captive. And if in covering the five miles to Judge Van Vorst's he exceeded the speed limit, the fact that from the rear seat Jimmie held the shotgun against the base of his skull was an extenuating circumstance.

They arrived in the nick of time. In his own car young
Van Vorst and a bag of golf clubs were just drawing away
from the house. Seeing the car climbing the steep driveway
that for a half mile led from his lodge to his front door, and
seeing Jimmie standing in the tonneau brandishing a gun,
the Judge hastily descended. The sight of the spy hunter
filled him with misgiving, but the sight of *him* gave Jimmie
sweet relief. For a small boy arresting German spies is no
easy task. For Jimmie the strain was great. And now that he
knew he had successfully delivered him into the hands of
the law, Jimmie's heart rose with happiness. The added
presence of a butler of magnificent bearing and of an ath-
letic-looking chauffeur increased his sense of security.
Their presence seemed to afford a feeling of security to
the prisoner also. As he brought the car to a halt, he
breathed a sigh. It was a sigh of deep relief.

Jimmie fell from the tonneau. In concealing his sense of
triumph, he was not entirely successful.

"I got him!" he cried. "I didn't make a mistake about this
one!"

"What one?" demanded Van Vorst.

Jimmie pointed dramatically at his prisoner. With an
anxious expression the stranger was tenderly fingering the
back of his head. He seemed to wish to assure himself that
it was still there.

"That one!" cried Jimmie. "He's a German spy!"

The patience of Judge Van Vorst fell from him. In his exclamation was indignation, anger, reproach.

"Jimmie!" he cried.

Jimmie thrust into his hand the map. It was his *Exhibit A.*
"Look what he's wrote," commanded the Scout. "It's all
military words. And these are his glasses. I took 'em off him.
They're made in Germany! I been stalking him for a week.
He's a spy!"

When Jimmie thrust the map before his face, Von Vorst

had glanced at it. Then he regarded it more closely. As he raised his eyes they showed that he was puzzled.

But he greeted the prisoner politely.

"I'm extremely sorry you've been annoyed," he said. "I'm only glad it's no worse. He might have shot you. He's mad over the idea that every stranger he sees—"

The prisoner quickly interrupted.

"Please!" he begged. "Don't blame the boy. He behaved extremely well. Might I speak with you—alone?" he asked.

Judge Von Vorst led the way across the terrace, and to the smoking room that served also as his office, and closed the door. The stranger walked directly to the mantelpiece and put his finger on a gold cup.

"I saw your mare win that at Belmont Park," he said. "She must have been a great loss to you?"

"She was," said Van Vorst. "The week before she broke her back, I refused three thousand for her. Will you have a cigarette?"

The stranger waved aside the cigarettes.

"I brought you inside," he said, "because I don't want your servants to hear; and because I don't want to hurt that boy's feelings. He's a fine boy; and he's a clever scout. I knew he was following me, and I threw him off twice, but today he caught me fair. If I really had been a German spy, I couldn't have got away from him. And I want him to think he has captured a German spy. Because he deserves just as much credit as though he had, and because it's best he shouldn't know whom he did capture."

Van Vorst pointed to the map. "My bet is," he said, "that you're an officer of the State militia, taking notes for the fall maneuvers. Am I right?"

The stranger smiled in approval, but shook his head.

"You're warm," he said, "but it's more serious than maneuvers. It's the Real Thing." From his pocketbook he took a visiting card and laid it on the table. "I'm Sherry McCoy," he said, "Captain of Artillery in the United States Army." He nodded to the hand telephone on the table.

"You can call up Governor's Island and get General Wood or his aide, Captain Dorey, on the phone. They sent me here. Ask them. I'm not picking out gun sites for the Germans; I'm picking out positions of defense for Americans when the Germans come!"

Van Vorst laughed derisively.

"My word!" he exclaimed. "You're as bad as Jimmie!"

Captain McCoy regarded him with disfavor.

"And you, sir," he retorted, "are as bad as ninety million other Americans. You won't believe! When the Germans are shelling this hill, when they're taking your hunters to pull their cook wagons, maybe you'll believe then."

"Are you serious?" demanded Van Vorst. "And you an army officer?"

"That's why I am serious," returned McCoy. "We know. But when we try to prepare for what is coming, we must do it secretly, in underhand ways, for fear the newspapers will get hold of it and ridicule us, and accuse us of trying to drag the country into war. That's why we have to prepare under cover. That's why I've had to skulk around these hills like a chicken thief. And," he added sharply, "that's why that boy must not know who I am. If he does, the General Staff will get a calling down at Washington, and I'll have my ears boxed."

Van Vorst moved to the door.

"He will never learn the truth from me," he said. "For I will tell him you are to be shot at sunrise."

"Good!" The captain laughed. "And tell me his name. If ever we fight over Westchester County, I want that lad for my chief of scouts. And give him this. Tell him to buy a new Scout uniform. Tell him it comes from you."

But no money could reconcile Jimmie to the sentence imposed upon his captive. He received the news with a howl of anguish. "You mustn't," he begged. "I never knowed you'd shoot him! I wouldn't have caught him, if I'd knowed that. I couldn't sleep if I thought he was going to be shot at sunrise." At the prospect of unending nightmares Jimmie's voice shook with terror. "Make it for twenty years," he begged. "Make it for ten," he coaxed, "but please, promise you won't shoot him."

When Van Vorst returned to Captain McCoy, he was smiling, and the butler who followed, bearing a tray and tinkling glasses, was trying not to smile.

"I gave Jimmie your ten dollars," said Van Vorst, "and made it twenty, and he has gone home. You will be glad to hear that he begged me to spare your life, and that your sentence has been commuted to twenty years in a fortress. I drink to your good fortune."

"No!" protested Captain McCoy. "We will drink to Jimmie."

When Captain McCoy had driven away, and his own car and the golf clubs had again been brought to the steps, Judge Van Vorst once more attempted to depart; but he was again delayed.

Other visitors were arriving.

Up the driveway a touring car approached, and though it limped on a flat tire, it approached at reckless speed. The two men in the front seat were white with dust; their faces, masked by automobile glasses, were indistinguishable. As though preparing for an immediate exit, the car swung in a circle until its nose pointed down the driveway up which it had just come. Raising his silk mask the one beside the driver shouted at Judge Van Vorst. His throat was parched, his voice was hoarse and hot with anger.

"A gray touring car," he shouted. "It stopped here. We saw it from that hill. Then the tire burst, and we lost our way. Where did he go?"

"Who?" demanded Van Vorst, stiffly. "Captain McCoy?"

The man exploded with an oath. The driver, with a shove of his elbow, silenced him.

"Yes, Captain McCoy," assented the driver eagerly. "Which way did he go?"

"To New York," said Van Vorst.

The driver shrieked at his companion.

"Then he's doubled back," he cried. "He's gone to New Haven." He stooped and threw in the clutch. The car lurched forward.

A cold terror swept young Van Vorst.

"What do you want with him?" he called. "Who are you?"

Over one shoulder the masked face glared at him. Above the roar of the car the words of the driver were flung back. "We're secret service from Washington," he shouted. "He's from their embassy. He's a German spy!"

Leaping and throbbing at sixty miles an hour, the car vanished in a curtain of white, whirling dust.

A SOURCE OF IRRITATION

STACY AUMONIER

To look at old Sam Gates you would never suspect him of having nerves. His sixty-nine years of close application to the needs of the soil had given him a certain earthy stolidity. To observe him hoeing, or thinning out a broad field of turnips, hardly attracted one's attention, he seemed so much part and parcel of the whole scheme. He blended into the soil like a glorified swede. Nevertheless, the half-dozen people who claimed his acquaintance knew him to be a man who suffered from little moods of irritability.

And on this glorious morning a little incident annoyed him unreasonably. It concerned his niece Aggie. She was a plump girl with clear, blue eyes, and a face inexpressive as the dumplings for which the county was famous. She came slowly across the long sweep of the downland and, putting down the bundle wrapped in a red handkerchief which contained his breakfast and dinner, she said: "Well, Uncle, is there any news?"

Now, this may not appear to the casual reader to be a remark likely to cause irritation, but it affected old Sam Gates as a very silly and unnecessary question. It was, moreover, the constant repetition of it which was beginning to anger him. He met his niece twice a day. In the morning she brought his bundle of food at seven, and when he passed his sister's cottage on the way home to tea at five she was invariably hanging about the gate, and she always said in the same voice: "Well, Uncle, is there any news?"

News! What news should there be? For sixty-nine years he had never lived farther than five miles from Halvesham. For nearly sixty of those years he had bent his back above the soil. There were, indeed, historic occasions. Once, for instance, when he had married Annie Hachet. And there was the birth of his daughter. There was also a famous occasion when he had visited London. Once he had been to a flower show at Market Roughborough. He either went or didn't go to church on Sundays. He had many interesting chats with Mr. James at the *Cowman,* and three years ago he had sold a pig to Mrs. Way. But he couldn't always have interesting news of this sort up his sleeve. Didn't the silly zany know that for the last three weeks he had been hoeing and thinning out turnips for Mr. Hodge on this very same field? What news could there be?

He blinked at his niece, and didn't answer. She undid the parcel and said, "Mrs. Goping's fowl got out again last night."

"Ah," he replied in a noncommittal manner and began to munch his bread and bacon. His niece picked up the handkerchief and, humming to herself, walked back across the field.

It was a glorious morning, and a white sea mist added to

the promise of a hot day. He sat there munching, thinking of
nothing in particular, but gradually subsiding into a mood
of placid content. He noticed the back of Aggie disappear
in the distance. It was a mile to the cottage and a mile and
a half to Halvesham. Silly things, girls. They were all alike.
One had to make allowances. He dismissed her from his
thoughts, and took a long swig of tea out of a bottle. Insects
buzzed lazily. He tapped his pocket to assure himself that
his pouch of shag was there, and then he continued munching. When he had finished, he lighted his pipe and
stretched himself comfortably. He looked along the line of
turnips he had thinned and then across the adjoining field
of swedes. Silver streaks appeared on the sea below the mist.
In some dim way he felt happy in his solitude amidst this
sweeping immensity of earth and sea and sky.

And then something else came to irritate him; it was one
of those dratted "airyplanes." "Airyplanes" were his pet
aversion. He could find nothing to be said in their favor.
Nasty, noisy, disfiguring things that seared the heavens and
made the earth dangerous. And every day there seemed to
be more and more of them. Of course this old war was responsible for a lot of them, he knew. The war was a plaguy
nuisance. They were shorthanded on the farm, beer and
tobacco were dear, and Mrs. Steven's nephew had been
and got wounded in the foot.

He turned his attention once more to the turnips; but an
"airyplane" has an annoying genius for gripping one's attention. When it appears on the scene, however much we
dislike it, it has a way of taking the stage center. We cannot
help constantly looking at it. And so it was with old Sam
Gates. He spat on his hands and blinked up at the sky. And
suddenly the airplane behaved in a very extraordinary manner. It was well over the sea when it seemed to lurch drunkenly and skimmed the water. Then it shot up at a dangerous

angle and zigzagged. It started to go farther out, and then turned and made for the land. The engines were making a curious grating noise. It rose once more, and then suddenly dived downward, and came plump down right in the middle of Mr. Hodge's field of swedes.

And then, as if not content with this desecration, it ran along the ground, ripping and tearing up twenty-five yards of good swedes, and then came to a stop.

Old Sam Gates was in a terrible state. The airplane was more than a hundred yards away, but he waved his arms and called out, "Hi, you there, you mustn't land in the swedes! They're Mr. Hodge's."

The instant the airplane stopped, a man leaped out and looked quickly around. He glanced at Sam Gates, and seemed uncertain whether to address him or whether to concentrate his attention on the flying machine. The latter arrangement appeared to be his ultimate decision. He dived under the engine and became frantically busy. Sam had never seen anyone work with such furious energy; but all the same it was not to be tolerated. It was disgraceful. Sam started out across the field, almost hurrying in his indignation. When he appeared within earshot of the aviator he cried out again: "Hi! You mustn't rest your old airyplane here! You've kicked up all Mr. Hodge's swedes. A nice thing you've done!"

He was within five yards when suddenly the aviator turned and covered him with a revolver! And speaking in a sharp, staccato voice, he said, "Old Grandfather, you must sit down. I am very much occupied. If you interfere or attempt to go away, I shoot you. So!"

Sam gazed at the horrid, glittering little barrel and gasped. Well, he never! To be threatened with murder when you're doing your duty in your employer's private property! But, still, perhaps the man was mad. A man must be more or less mad to go up in one of those crazy things. And life was very sweet on that summer morning despite sixty-nine years. He sat down among the swedes.

The aviator was so busy with his cranks and machinery that he hardly deigned to pay him any attention except to keep the revolver handy. He worked feverishly, and Sam sat watching him. At the end of ten minutes he appeared to have solved his troubles with the machine, but he still seemed very scared. He kept on glancing round and out to sea. When his repairs were complete he straightened his back and wiped the perspiration from his brow. He was apparently on the point of springing back into the machine and going off when a sudden mood of facetiousness, caused by relief from the strain he had endured, came to him. He turned to old Sam and smiled, at the same time remarking, "Well, old Grandfather, and now we shall be all right, isn't it?"

He came close up to Sam, and then suddenly started back.

"*Gott!*" he cried. "Paul Jouperts!"

Bewildered, Sam gazed at him, and the madman started talking to him in some foreign tongue. Sam shook his head.

"You've no right," he remarked, "to come barging through the swedes of Mr. Hodge's."

And then the aviator behaved in a most peculiar manner. He came up and examined Sam's face very closely, and gave a sudden tug at his beard and hair, as if to see whether they were real or false.

"What is your name, old man?" he said.

"Sam Gates."

The aviator muttered some words that sounded something like "mare vudish," and then turned to his machine. He appeared to be dazed and in a great state of doubt. He fumbled with some cranks, but kept glancing at old Sam. At last he got into the car and strapped himself in. Then he stopped, and sat there deep in thought. At last he suddenly unstrapped himself and sprang out again and, approaching Sam, said very deliberately, "Old Grandfather, I shall require you to accompany me."

Sam gasped. "Eh!" he said. "What be you talkin' about? 'Company? I got these here lines o' turnips—I be already behind—" The disgusting little revolver once more flashed before his eyes.

"There must be no discussion," came the voice. "It is necessary that you mount the seat of the car without delay. Otherwise I shoot you like the dog you are. So!"

Old Sam was hale and hearty. He had no desire to die so ignominiously. The pleasant smell of the Norfolk downland was in his nostrils; his foot was on his native heath. He mounted the seat of the car, contenting himself with a mutter. "Well, that be a nice thing, I must say! Flyin' about the country with all the turnips only half thinned!"

He found himself strapped in. The aviator was in a fever of anxiety to get away. The engines made a ghastly sputter and noise. The thing started running along the ground. Suddenly it shot upward, giving the swedes a last contemptuous kick. At twenty minutes to eight that morning old Sam found himself being borne right up above his fields and out to sea! His breath came quickly. He was a little frightened.

The thing was so fantastic and sudden that his mind could not grasp it. He only felt in some vague way that he was going to die, and he struggled to attune his mind to the change. He offered up a mild prayer to God, Who, he felt, must be very near, somewhere up in these clouds. Automatically he thought of the vicar at Halvesham, and a certain sense of comfort came to him at the reflection that on the previous day he had taken a "cooking of runner beans" to God's representative in that village. He felt calmer after that, but the horrid machine seemed to go higher and higher. He could not turn in his seat and he could see noth-

ing but sea and sky. Of course the man was mad, mad as a
March hare. Of what earthly use could *he* be to any one?
Besides, he had talked pure gibberish, and called him Paul
something, when he had already told him that his name was
Sam. The thing would fall down into the sea soon, and they
would both be drowned. Well, well, he had almost reached
three-score years and ten. He was protected by a screen,
but it seemed very cold. What on earth would Mr. Hodge
say? There was no one left to work the land but a fool of a
boy named Billy Whitehead at Dene's Cross. On, on, on
they went at a furious pace. His thoughts danced discon-
nectedly from incidents of his youth, conversations with
the vicar, hearty meals in the open, a frock his sister wore
on the day of the postman's wedding, the drone of a psalm,
the illness of some ewes belonging to Mr. Hodge. Everything seemed to be moving very rapidly, upsetting his sense
of time. He felt outraged, and yet at moments there was
something entrancing in the wild experience. He seemed to
be living at an incredible pace. Perhaps he was really dead
and on his way to the kingdom of God. Perhaps this was the
way they took people.

After some indefinite period he suddenly caught sight
of a long strip of land. Was this a foreign country, or were
they returning? He had by this time lost all feeling of fear.
He became interested and almost disappointed. The "airyplane" was not such a fool as it looked. It was very wonderful to be right up in the sky like this. His dreams were suddenly disturbed by a fearful noise. He thought the machine
was blown to pieces. It dived and ducked through the air,
and things were bursting all round it and making an awful
din, and then it went up higher and higher. After a while
these noises ceased, and he felt the machine gliding downward. They were really right above solid land—trees, fields,
streams, and white villages. Down, down, down they glided.
This was a foreign country. There were straight avenues of

poplars and canals. This was not Halvesham. He felt the thing glide gently and bump into a field. Some men ran forward and approached them, and the mad aviator called out to them. They were mostly fat men in gray uniforms, and they all spoke this foreign gibberish. Someone came and unstrapped him. He was very stiff and could hardly move. An exceptionally gross-looking man punched him in the ribs and roared with laughter. They all stood round and laughed at him, while the mad aviator talked to them and kept pointing at him. Then he said, "Old Grandfather, you must come with me."

He was led to an iron-roofed building and shut in a little room. There were guards outside with fixed bayonets. After a while the mad aviator appeared again, accompanied by two soldiers. He beckoned him to follow. They marched through a quadrangle and entered another building. They went straight into an office where a very important-looking man, covered with medals, sat in an easy chair. There was a lot of saluting and clicking of heels. The aviator pointed at Sam and said something, and the man with the medals started at sight of him, and then came up and spoke to him in English.

"What is your name? Where do you come from? Your age? The name and birthplace of your parents?"

He seemed intensely interested, and also pulled his hair and beard to see if they came off. So well and naturally did he and the aviator speak English that after a voluble examination they drew apart, and continued the conversation in that language. And the extraordinary conversation was of this nature:

"It is a most remarkable resemblance," said the man with medals. "*Unglaublich!* But what do you want me to do with him, Hausemann?"

"The idea came to me suddenly, Excellency," replied the aviator, "and you may consider it worthless. It is just this.

The resemblance is so amazing. Paul Jouperts has given us more valuable information than anyone at present in our service, and the English know that. There is an award of five thousand francs on his head. Twice they have captured him, and each time he escaped. All the company commanders and their staff have his photograph. He is a serious thorn in their flesh."

"Well?" replied the man with the medals.

The aviator whispered confidentially, "Suppose, your Excellency, that they found the dead body of Paul Jouperts"

"Well?" replied the big man.

"My suggestion is this. Tomorrow, as you know, the English are attacking Hill 701, which for tactical reasons we have decided to evacuate. If after the attack they find the dead body of Paul Jouperts in, say, the second line, they will take no further trouble in the matter. You know their lack of thoroughness. Pardon me, I was two years at Oxford University. And consequently Paul Jouperts will be able to prosecute his labors undisturbed."

The man with the medals twirled his mustache and looked thoughtfully at his colleague.

"Where is Paul at the moment?" he asked.

"He is acting as a gardener at the Convent of St. Eloise, at Mailleton-en-haut, which, as you know, is one hundred meters from the headquarters of the British central army staff."

The man with the medals took two or three rapid turns up and down the room, then he said, "Your plan is excellent, Hausemann. The only point of difficulty is that the attack started this morning."

"This morning?" exclaimed the other.

"Yes. The English attacked unexpectedly at dawn. We have already evacuated the first line. We shall evacuate the second line at eleven-fifty. It is now ten-fifteen. There may be just time."

He looked suddenly at old Sam in the way that a butcher might look at a prize heifer at an agricultural show and remarked casually, "Yes, it is a remarkable resemblance. It seems a pity not to—do something with it."

Then, speaking in German, he added, "It is worth trying. And if it suceeds the higher authorities shall hear of your lucky accident and inspiration, Herr Hausemann. Instruct *Ober-leutenant* Schultz to send the old fool by two orderlies to the east extremity of Trench 38. Keep him there till the order of evacuation is given, then shoot him, but don't disfigure him, and lay him out face upward."

The aviator saluted and withdrew, accompanied by his victim. Old Sam had not understood the latter part of the conversation, and he did not catch quite all that was said in English, but he felt that somehow things were not becoming too promising, and it was time to assert himself. So he remarked when they got outside, "Now, look here, Mister, when am I goin' to get back to my turnips?"

And the aviator replied, with a pleasant smile, "Do not be disturbed, old Grandfather. You shall get back to the soil quite soon."

In a few moments he found himself in a large gray car, accompanied by four soldiers. The aviator left him. The country was barren and horrible, full of great pits and rents, and he could hear the roar of the artillery and the shriek of shells. Overhead, airplanes were buzzing angrily. He seemed to be suddenly transported from the kingdom of God to the pit of darkness. He wondered whether the vicar had enjoyed the runner beans. He could not imagine runner beans growing here; runner beans, aye, or anything else. If this was a foreign country, give him dear old England!

Gr-r! bang! Something exploded just at the rear of the

car. The soldiers ducked, and one of them pushed him in
the stomach and swore.

"An ugly-looking lout," he thought. "If I were twenty
years younger, I'd give him a punch in the eye that'd make
him sit up."

The car came to a halt by a broken wall. The party hurried out and dived behind a mound. He was pulled down a
kind of shaft, and found himself in a room buried right underground, where three officers were drinking and smoking.
The soldiers saluted and handed them a typewritten dis-
patch. The officers looked at him drunkenly, and one came
up and pulled his beard and spat in his face and called him
"an old English swine." He then shouted out some instructions to the soldiers, and they led Sam out into the narrow
trench. One walked behind him, and occasionally prodded
him with the butt end of a gun. The trenches were half full
of water and reeked of gases, powder, and decaying matter.
Shells were constantly bursting overhead, and in places the
trenches had crumbled and were nearly blocked up. They
stumbled on, sometimes falling, sometimes dodging moving
masses, and occasionally crawling over the dead bodies of
men. At last they reached a deserted-looking trench, and
one of the soldiers pushed him into the corner of it and
growled something, and then disappeared round the angle.
Old Sam was exhausted. He leaned panting against the mud
wall, expecting every minute to be blown to pieces by one
of those infernal things that seemed to be getting more and
more insistent. The din went on for nearly twenty minutes,
and he was alone in the trench. He fancied he heard a
whistle amidst the din. Suddenly one of the soldiers who
had accompanied him came stealthily round the corner,
and there was a look in his eye old Sam did not like. When he
was within five yards the soldier raised his rifle and pointed
it at Sam's body. Some instinct impelled the old man at that
instant to throw himself forward on his face. As he did so he

was aware of a terrible explosion, and he had just time to observe the soldier falling in a heap near him, and then he lost consciousness.

His consciousness appeared to return to him with a snap. He was lying on a plank in a building, and he heard someone say, "I believe the old boy's English."

He looked around. There were a lot of men lying there, and others in khaki and white overalls were busy among them. He sat up, rubbed his head, and said, "Hi, Mister, where be I now?"

Someone laughed, and a young man came up and said, "Well, old man, you were very nearly done for. Who are you?"

Someone came up, and two of them were discussing him. One of them said, "He's quite all right. He was only knocked out. Better take him in to the colonel. He may be a spy."

The other came up, touched his shoulder, and remarked, "Can you walk, Uncle?"

He replied, "Aye, I can walk all right."

"That's an old sport!"

The young man took his arm and helped him out of the room into a courtyard. They entered another room, where an elderly, kind-faced officer was seated at a desk. The officer looked up and exclaimed, "Good Heavens! Bradshaw, do you know who you've got there?"

The younger one said, "No. Who, sir?"

"It's Paul Jouperts!" exclaimed the colonel.

"Paul Jouperts! Great Scott!"

The older officer addressed himself to Sam. He said, "Well, we've got you once more, Paul. We shall have to be a little more careful this time."

The young officer said, "Shall I detail a squad, sir?"

"We can't shoot him without a court-martial," replied the kind-faced senior.

Then Sam interpolated, "Look here, sir, I'm fair sick of all this. My name bean't Paul. My name's Sam. I was a-thinnin' a line o' turnips—"

Both officers burst out laughing, and the younger one said, "Good! Very good! Isn't it amazing, sir, the way they not only learn the language, but even take the trouble to learn a dialect!"

The older man busied himself with some papers.

"Well, Sam," he remarked, "you shall be given a chance to prove your identity. Our methods are less drastic than those of your Boche masters. What part of England are you supposed to come from? Let's see how much you can bluff us with your topographical knowledge."

"I was a-thinnin' a line o' turnips this mornin' at half-past seven on Mr. Hodge's farm at Halvesham when one o' these airyplanes came down among the swedes. I tells him to get clear o' that, when the feller what gets out o' the car he draws a revolver and he says, 'you must 'company I—' "

"Yes, yes," interrupted the senior officer, "that's all very good. Now tell me—where is Halvesham? What is the name of the local vicar? I'm sure you'd know that."

Old Sam rubbed his chin.

"I sits under the Reverend David Pryce, Mister, and a good, God-fearin' man he be. I took him a cookin' o' runner beans only yesterday. I works for Mr. Hodge, what owns Greenway Manor and has a stud farm at Newmarket, they say."

"Charles Hodge?" asked the young officer.

"Aye, Charlie Hodge. You write and ask him if he knows old Sam Gates."

The two officers looked at each other, and the older one looked at Sam more closely.

"It's very extraordinary," he remarked.

"Everybody knows Charlie Hodge," added the younger officer.

It was at that moment that a wave of genius swept over old Sam. He put his hand to his head and suddenly jerked out:

"What's more, I can tell you where this here Paul is. He's actin' as gardener in a convent. . . ." He puckered up his brows, fumbled with his hat, and then got out, "Mighten-o."

The older officer gasped.

"Mailleton-en-haut! Good Heavens! What makes you say that, old man?"

Sam tried to give an account of his experience and the things he had heard said by the German officers; but he was getting tired, and he broke off in the middle to say, "Ya haven't a bite o' somethin' to eat, I suppose, Mister; or a glass o' beer? I usually has my dinner at twelve o'clock."

Both the officers laughed, and the older said, "Get him some food, Bradshaw, and a bottle of beer from the mess. We'll keep this old man here. He interests me."

While the younger man was doing this, the chief pressed a button and summoned another junior officer.

"Gateshead," he remarked, "ring up the GHQ. and instruct them to arrest the gardener in that convent at the top of the hill and then to report."

The officer saluted and went out, and in a few minutes a tray of hot food and a large bottle of beer were brought to the old man, and he was left alone in the corner of the room to negotiate his welcome compensation. And in the execution he did himself and his country credit. In the meanwhile the officers were very busy. People were coming and going and examining maps, and telephone bells were ringing furiously. They did not disturb old Sam's gastric operations. He cleaned up the mess tins and finished the last drop of beer. The senior officer found time to offer him a cigarette, but he replied, "Thank you kindly, sir, but I'd rather smoke my pipe."

The colonel smiled and said, "Oh, all right, smoke away."

He lighted up, and the fumes of the shag permeated the room. Someone opened another window, and the young officer who had addressed him at first suddenly looked at him and exclaimed, "He's innocent! You couldn't get shag like that anywhere but in Norfolk."

It must have been an hour later when another officer entered and saluted.

"Message from the GHQ., sir," he said.

"Well?"

"They have arrested the gardener at the convent of St. Eloise, and they have every reason to believe that he is the notorious Paul Jouperts."

The colonel stood up, and his eyes beamed. He came over to old Sam and shook his hand.

"Mr. Gates," he said, "you are an old brick. You will hear more of this. You have probably been the means of delivering something very useful into our hands. Your own honor is vindicated. A loving Government will probably award you five shillings or a Victoria Cross or something of that sort. In the meantime, what can I do for you?"

Old Sam scratched his chin. "I want to get back home," he said.

"Well, even that might be arranged."

"I want to get back home in time for tea."

"What time do you have tea?"

"Five o'clock or thereabouts."

"I see."

A kindly smile came into the eyes of the colonel. He turned to another officer standing by the table and said, "Raikes, is any one going across this afternoon with dispatches?"

"Yes, sir," replied the other officer. "Commander Jennings is leaving at three o'clock."

"You might ask him if he could see me."

Within ten minutes a young man in a flight-commander's uniform entered.

"Ah, Jennings," said the colonel, "here is a little affair which concerns the honor of the British army. My friend here, Sam Gates, has come over from Halvesham, in Norfolk, in order to give us valuable information. I have promised him that he shall get home to tea at five o'clock. Can you take a passenger?"

The young man threw back his head and laughed.

"Lord!" he exclaimed. "What an old sport! Yes, I expect I can manage it. Where is the godforsaken place?"

A large ordnance map of Norfolk (which had been captured from a German officer) was produced, and the young man studied it closely.

At three o'clock precisely old Sam, finding himself something of a hero and quite glad to escape from the embarrassment which the position entailed upon him, once more sped skyward in a dratted "airyplane."

At twenty minutes to five he landed once more among Mr. Hodge's swedes. The breezy young airman shook hands with him and departed inland. Old Sam sat down and surveyed the familiar field of turnips.

"A nice thing, I must say!" he muttered to himself as he looked along the lines of unthinned turnips. He still had twenty minutes, and so he went slowly along and completed a line which he had begun in the morning. He then deliberately packed up his dinner things and his tools and started for home.

As he came round the corner of Stillway's meadow and the cottage came in view, his niece stepped out of the copse with a basket on her arm.

"Well, Uncle," she said, "is there any news?"

It was then that old Sam really lost his temper.

"News!" he said. "News! Drat the girl! What news should there be? Sixty-nine year' I live in these here parts, hoein' and weedin' and thinnin', and mindin' Charlie Hodge's sheep. Am I one o' these here storybook folk havin' news happen to me all the time? Ain't it enough, you silly, dab-faced zany, to earn enough to buy a bite o' something to eat and a glass o' beer and a place to rest your head o' night without always wantin' news, news, news! I tell you it's this that leads you to half the troubles in the world. Devil take the news!"

And turning his back on her, he went fuming up the hill.

INTELLIGENCE

C. S. FORESTER

Capt. George Crowe, C.B., D.S.O., R.N., walked down three short steps into the blinding sunshine that made the big airplane's wings seem to waver in reflected light. The heat of the Potomac Valley hit him in the face, a sweltering contrast to the air-cooled comfort of the plane. He was wearing a blue uniform more suitable for the bridge of a destroyer than for the damp heat of Washington, and that was not very surprising, because not a great many hours earlier he had been on the bridge of a destroyer, and most of these hours he had spent in airplanes, sitting in miserable discomfort at first, breathing through his oxygen mask in the plane that had brought him across the Atlantic, and then reclining in cushioned ease in the passenger plane that had brought him from his point of landing here.

The United States naval officer who had been sent to meet him had no difficulty in picking him out—the four gold stripes on his sleeves and the ribbons on his chest marked him out, even if his bulk and his purposeful carriage had not done so.

"Captain Crowe?" asked the naval lieutenant.

"Yes."

"Glad to see you, sir. My name's Harley."

The two shook hands.

"I have a car waiting, sir," Harley went on. "They're expecting you at the Navy Department, if you wouldn't mind coming at once."

The car swung out of the airport and headed for the bridge while Crowe blinked round him. It was a good deal of a contrast—two days before he had been with his flotilla, refueling in a home port; then had come the summons to the Admiralty, a fleeting glimpse of wartime London, and now here he was in the District of Columbia, United States of America, with the chances of sudden death infinitely removed, shops plentifully stocked, motorcars still swarming, and the city of Washington spread out before him.

Crowe stirred a little uneasily. He hoped he had not been brought to this land of plenty unnecessarily; he regretted already having left his flotilla and the eternal hunt after U-boats.

The car stopped and Harley sprang out and held the door open for him. There were guards in naval uniform round the door, revolvers sagging at their thighs; a desk at which they paused for a space.

"No exceptions." Harley smiled, apologizing for the fact that not even the uniform of a British naval captain would let them into the holy of holies for which they were headed. There were two men in the room to which Harley led him.

"Good morning," said the admiral.

"Good morning, sir," said Crowe.

"Sorry to hurry you like this," the admiral said gruffly. "But it's urgent. Meet Lieutenant Brand."

Brand was in plain clothes—seedy plain clothes. Crowe puzzled over them. Those clothes were the sort of suit that a middle-class Frenchman, not too well off, and the father of a family, would wear. And Brand's face was marked with weariness and anxiety.

"Brand left Lisbon about the same time you left London," said the admiral. His eyes twinkled—no, *twinkled* was too gentle a word—they glittered under thick black eyebrows. No man who looked into those eyes even for a moment would want to be the admiral's enemy. Now he shot a direct glance at Crowe, twisted his thin lips, and shot a question.

"Supposing," he asked, "you had the chance to give orders to a U-boat captain, what orders would you give?"

Crowe kept his face expressionless. "That would depend," he said cautiously, "on who the U-boat captain was."

"In this case it is *Korvettenkapitän* Lothar Wolfgang von und zu Loewenstein."

Captain Crowe repressed a start. "I know him," he said.

"That's why you're here." The admiral grinned. "Didn't they tell you in London? You're here because few people on our side of the ocean know Loewenstein better than you."

Crowe considered. Yes, he decided, the admiral's statement was right. He knew Loewenstein. In the year before 1939, the German had made quite a reputation for himself by his bold handling of his yacht in English regattas—Loewenstein and his helmsman. Burke? Of course not. Bruch—Burch—something like that. Good man, that helmsman.

Crowe had met Loewenstein on several formal occasions when the British navy had met detachments of the German navy while visiting. And since 1939 their paths had crossed more than once—Crowe on the surface in his destroyer, and Loewenstein 200 feet below in his submarine.

"Loewenstein," the admiral was saying, "left Bordeaux on the thirteenth—that's four days ago—with orders to operate

on the Atlantic Coast. We know he has four other U-boats
with him. Five in all."

The shaggy-browed admiral leaned over the desk. "And
Loewenstein is out to get the *Queen Anne.*"

Captain Crowe blinked again.

"The *Queen Anne,*" pursued the American admiral ruth-
lessly, "that is due to clear very shortly with men for the
Middle East and India. Men we can't afford to lose. Not to
mention the ship herself."

"What's the source of your information, sir?" Captain
Crowe asked.

"Brand here," said the admiral, "also left Bordeaux on the
thirteenth."

That piece of news stiffened Crowe in his chair, and he
stared more closely at the lieutenant in plain clothes. The
news explained a lot—the seedy French suit, the hollow
cheeks and the haggard expression. A man who had been
acting as a spy in Bordeaux for the last six months would
naturally look haggard.

Brand spoke for the first time and his pleasant Texan
drawl carried even more than the hint that he had not only
been speaking French but thinking in French for a long
time.

"This is what I brought from Bordeaux," he said, taking
an untidy bundle of papers from the admiral's desk. "It's
the code the German agents in this country use for com-
munications with the U-boats."

Crowe took the bundle from his hand and gave it a cur-
sory glance. This was not the time to give it prolonged
study, complicated as it was, and half the columns were in
German, which he did not understand. The other half were
in English, and were composed of a curiously arbitrary se-
quence of words. Crowe caught sight of "galvanized iron
buckets," and "canned lobster" and "ripe avocados." Farther down the column there were figures instead of words—

apparently every value in American money from a cent to five dollars had a German equivalent, and the words *pounds* and *dozens* and even the hours of the day could convey certain meanings when put in their proper context.

"With that code," explained Brand, "you can give time, courses, latitude and longitude—anything you want."

Crowe braved a question he half suspected he should not have asked. "Where did you get this?"

"It's not the original," interposed the admiral. "The Nazis don't know we've got this. There's no missing original to give them the tip to change their code."

"A French girl got it for me," Brand explained.

There was a silence and then the admiral said, "Well, captain, there's the setup. What have you got to suggest?"

Captain Crowe looked down at the floor and then up at the admiral.

"Of course the *Queen Anne* will be secured by convoy," he said. "I know you're not thinking of letting her make her regular transport run without escort. If Loewenstein is waiting for her with five submarines, her speed won't do her any good. And if the Germans know the course and time out of your ports now, there's no guaranteeing they won't know any change in course or time you might give the *Queen Anne*."

The admiral made a sudden gesture. "We can send the *Queen* out with half the fleet," he said. "But once we're at. . . . Map, please, lientenant!"

Young Harley spread a map in front of the admiral. Captain Crowe hunched over it, following the line pointed by the top striper's finger.

"Once there," said the admiral, "we'll have to let the *Queen* go on her own. We can't go past that point without neglecting our coastal duties. And Loewenstein is bound to trail along until the escort leaves. Then he'll hit. Unless he can be drawn off."

"Yes," echoed Crowe absently. "Unless we can draw him off."

"Can we?" the admiral demanded. "Or—I'm sorry—that's an unfair question, thrown at you all at once, Captain. Think it over and tomorrow morning at"—he glanced at his wristwatch—"ten we'll talk it over."

"It wouldn't break my heart," said the naval-intelligence agent, Brand, suddenly, "if something drastic happened to Loewenstein. I've seen some of the pictures he's taken with his little camera from conning towers. Close-ups of drowning men—and one that's the pride of his collection, a woman and kid off the *Athenia*."

"Something drastic is going to happen to Loewenstein," said the admiral. He looked at Crowe, and the captain blinked.

"Righto," said Captain Crowe.

He found himself outside the office without clearly realizing how he got there. He wanted to walk; he was urgently anxious to walk, partly because long hours in planes had cramped his legs—legs accustomed to miles of deck marching—and partly because he wanted to think—had to think—and he thought best on his feet.

He had to draw Loewenstein off. But what could draw a sub commander off a prize like the *Queen Anne*? To sink the *Queen* would give any U-boat skipper the *Pour le Merite* with oak leaves or whatever brand of decoration Hitler was giving out now. A man would have to be mad to forsake a prize like that. Mad or—but Loewenstein had been half mad that day he had seized the wheel from his helmsman at that Copenhagen regatta and had tried to ram the boat that had overhauled him and blanketed him, stealing the race at the last moment. That Danish club had disbarred Loewenstein for that. But the helmsman had been exonerated. Good man, that helmsman, Crowe thought.

Braucht—it was something that started with a *B*. Broening. Yes, that was it, Broening.

Crowe looked around him, squinted at the sun, tucked his chin in his limp white collar and set off boldly in the direction of the British embassy. He was remembering all he could about *Korvettenkapitän* von und zu Loewenstein. He called up the slightly pug nose, the cold blue eyes, the colorless hair slicked back from the forehead; he remembered all these. Then there was the ruthless boldness with which he would jockey for position at the start of a yacht race. He would bear down on another boat, keeping his course while the helmsman, Broening, yelled a warning until the other boat fell off. The protest flags fluttered on many occasions when Loewenstein sailed. And after the races, it always was Loewenstein and some beautiful harpy at their table, alone, except for the miserable helmsman, Broening. Now, Loewenstein was the boldest of all U-boat captains.

Crowe knew his lips were not moving, but his mind was speaking. Draw Loewenstein off, it said. But how? Loewenstein is a believer in the gun, as shown by his record. He conserves his torpedoes to the last. The ideal method of attack, according to Loewenstein, is to rise to the surface at night, preferably when there is just enough moon, or shore-light glare, to give a good silhouette of the target. He times his rise so that the convoy is almost upon him. Then he uses his guns furiously, pumping shells into every hull he can see; his whole pack of U-boats firing together. Then, before the escort comes up, even before the deck guns of the freighters can go into action, his sub flotilla submerges and scatters on divergent courses that confuse surface listening posts so that the escort destroyers don't know the exact spot over which to make their run. Very clever—except he thinks the Americans don't know how he works. And I—God help me—have been brought over here to show Loewenstein he guessed wrong. But what is it about Broening that's so important? Why do I keep thinking about him?

It would be eight or nine days before Loewenstein and his pack could be expected off the American coast. In that time the moon would be past its full. Three quarters, rising about eleven. So that it might be best to. . . .

Crowe forgot the sweat that dripped down his face—everything except the problem at hand. It was something that even in his wide experience he had not encountered before, this opportunity of sending orders to an enemy in the sure and certain knowledge that they would be received and acted upon.

Broening, he told himself. Last I heard of him was that he'd become a johnny-come-lately in the Nazi party and Von Ribbentrop had sent him to some little Latin-American country as a consul. Loewenstein must have loved that. Always hated the man, Loewenstein did, even though he won races for him. Now, despite all Loewenstein's Junker background, it seems that Broening is outstripping him in the race for prestige. I'll wager Loewenstein would like nothing better than to. . . . I believe I have it.

The shower bath offered him by a friend at the embassy was something for which he would have given a month's pay. He stepped under the cold rain and pranced about solemnly while the healing water washed away the heat and his irritation. A plan to deal with Loewenstein was forming in his mind, and as he cooled down, his spirits rose until he nearly began to sing, until he remembered that he was on the dignified premises of the British embassy. But he still grew happier and happier until he was struck by a fresh realization. Then his spirits fell abruptly. He had not written either to Susan or Dorothy this week, thanks to the hours spent traveling from England. And today was nearly over, and tomorrow he would have to write to Miriam—three letters pressing on him, to say nothing of the official report he would have to write. Crowe groaned and stayed under the shower a minute longer than he need have done in order to postpone the evil moment when he would have to come out and face a world in which letters had to be written, and when he did he was cursing himself for a softhearted fool for not cutting off the correspondence and saving himself a great deal of trouble.

But outside, the assistant naval attaché welcomed him with a smile.

"Here's Miss Haycraft," he said. "I thought you'd like her assistance in writing your report. You needn't worry about her—she knows more secrets than the admiralty itself."

Miss Haycraft was a pleasant little fair-haired thing with an unobtrusive air of complete efficiency. She sat down with her notebook in just the right way to start Crowe off pouring out his report of his interview with the admiral and Lieutenant Brand.

Halfway through his discourse, Captain Crowe stopped. "I wonder if the embassy has any records on a man named Broening?" he asked. "Nazi fellow. Believe he was consul or minister or something in a Central American state. I. . . ."

"Yes, Captain," said Miss Haycraft crisply. "*Herr* Broening is in New York, waiting to take passage on the diplo-matic-exchange ship, *Frottingholm*."

"Ah?" asked Crowe. "And when does the *Frottingholm* sail?"

"It's not definite," the girl answered. "There's some trouble getting Berlin to assure safe passage."

"Umm," said Captain Crowe.

In another ten minutes the report was done. Crowe looked at Miss Haycraft and felt temptation; not temptation with regard to Miss Haycraft, however; she was not the girl to offer it.

"Was the A. N. A. really speaking the truth when he said you could be trusted with a secret?" he asked.

"Yes," said Miss Haycraft, and her manner implied that there was no need at all to enlarge on the subject.

"All right then," said Crowe, taking the plunge. "Take this letter. 'Dear Susan: As you will see, I have got hold of a typewriter, and I am trying my hand at it. Please forgive me this week for being so impersonal, but I have had a good deal to do. I wish you could guess where I am now; all I can say is I wish you were here with me because. . . .' "

The letter to Susan ran off as smoothly as oil; it was even more impressive than the writing of the report. When it was finished, Crowe looked at Miss Haycraft once more. Well, he might as well be hanged for sheep as for lamb.

"I'd like you," he said, "to do that letter over three times —no, you might as well make it four. Begin 'em 'Dear Susan,' 'Dear Dorothy,' 'Dear Miriam,' and 'Dear Jane'—no, not 'Dear Jane.' You'd better say 'Dearest Jane.' Have you got that right?"

"Yes, Captain Crowe," said Miss Haycraft, and she did not even smile.

This was marvelous; his conscience was clear for a week, and Crowe felt more like singing than ever, but he had to restrain himself. He did not mind letting Miss Haycraft into the secret of his epistolary amours, but singing in front of her was another matter. Perhaps it was the mounting internal pressure arising from the suppression of his desire that led to the rapid evolution in his mind of the plan to discomfit Loewenstein.

All I need, he told himself, is an old hulk with a loose propeller shaft, a quick job of maritime face lifting, and some co-operation from the newspaper and wireless johnnies. I've a feeling the admiral ought to be able to get those things for me.

"What can I do for you, Mr. O'Connor?" asked the manager of the broadcasting station, after he had offered his unknown visitor a chair.

Mr. O'Connor displayed a badge held in the palm of his hand and passed an unsealed envelope across the desk to the manager.

"Very glad to do anything I can," said the head of the broadcasting station, when he read the enclosed letter.

Mr. O'Connor produced a couple of typewritten sheets of paper.

"That goes on the air," he said, "at eleven o'clock to-morrow morning, at Reitz's usual time."

The manager looked at the sheets. It was the usual kind of broadcast for which Mr. Reitz paid twice a week, advertising the goods for sale in his store—galvanized buckets at sixty-nine cents, Grade A canned peaches at thirty-nine cents, and so on. The turns of phrase, the arrangement of the wording bore the closest possible resemblance to Mr. Reitz's usual style.

"I suppose I'll have to do it," said the station manager. "Glad to do anything to help, as I said. But what is Reitz going to say when he hears it?"

"He may hear it," said O'Connor dryly, "but he won't be in a position to object. He'll be in a safe place, and I don't expect it'll be long before he's in a safer place still."

"I see," said the station manager.

There was nothing more to be said on the subject of Mr. Reitz's objections; it had all been said in those few words and in the glance of Mr. O'Connor's hard eyes.

"All the same," supplemented the FBI agent, "I would prefer it if you did not discuss Reitz with anyone else."

"Of course not," said the man across the desk. "And this will go on the air at eleven tomorrow morning."

"Thank you very much," said O'Connor, reaching for his hat.

"It will be a clear night, Captain," said the admiral, coming up to the tiny bridge. "That's the latest forecast."

"I wouldn't object to a bit of haze myself, sir," said Crowe.

"If you were in heaven," chuckled the admiral, "I'll bet you'd say your crown didn't fit and your harp was out of tune. But you must admit everything's come off slicker than an eel in a barrel of grease. There's the old *Peter Wilkes,* God bless her leaking hull, all dressed up in a coat of white paint and a big sign, *Diplomat,* on her side, lighted up like a Coney Island excursion boat, wallowing along ahead of us with that fake second funnel threatening to blow off any minute. And her loose screw is kicking up such a fuss that our listeners are going deaf. And here we are, seven of us, coasting along behind that makeshift *Frottingholm,* blacked out and with our men at battle stations. I only hope your hunch is right, Captain. I'd hate to lose that skeleton crew aboard the *Wilkes.* And I'd hate to have this whole expedition turn out to be a howler."

"It won't," said Crowe, with an assurance that he did not feel. "Loewenstein hates Broening—always has. He knows if his former helmsman gets back to Berlin safely, Raeder is due to give him a naval command that would put him over Loewenstein. And Germany wants to break up Pan-American solidarity if she can. What better way than to have a U-boat sink a diplomatic ship and claim it was done by you Americans or us British? Loewenstein thinks he can kill two birds with one stone—getting rid of a personal enemy and staging a *cause célèbre* at the same time. And he won't torpedo that ship. He's been told it's without escort, and he'll surface and shell, and machine-gun the lifeboats later, at his convenience."

"And the loose screw of the *Wilkes,*" observed the admiral, "will prevent his listeners from knowing we're in the neighborhood."

"Right, sir."

Crowe turned and looked back over the rigid line following behind them. He felt very happy at the imminent prospect of action. He was about to sing, when he remembered the presence of the admiral beside him. Admirals cramped one's style in a manner especially noticeable to a captain whose rank usually made him monarch of all he surveyed.

"Lord Jeffrey Amherst was a soldier of the King," sang the admiral, as if he were doing it just to rub in the difference in rank. Then be broke off. "You've no business here at all, you know."

"None, sir," agreed Crowe. "But I'm not the only one like that on board."

"Perhaps not." The admiral grinned.

The sun was down now and the darkness was increasing rapidly. The false-faced *Frottingholm* lurched and staggered in the rising seas, a boldly lighted figure on a darkening seascape. The destroyer which Crowe rode rose and fell to the long Atlantic rollers. The men were at the guns. Down below, there were men with earphones clamped over their heads, trying to pick out the sound of submarine engines beneath the howl of the *Wilkes'* clattering screw. The ship, the whole little squadron, was keyed up, ready to explode into action. Somewhere in the darkness ahead was Loewenstein, rereading, perhaps, the information that had come to him that morning regarding the sailing of the *Frottingholm* with one August Broening aboard, the course and speed and destination of the diplomatic-exchange ship. No one could be quite sure of how Loewenstein would act on that information, but everything that Crowe knew about him led the captain to believe he would attack on the surface, about midnight, with his prey silhouetted against a nearly level moon. And, Crowe hoped, Loewenstein would use his deck guns to carry away the radio antenna first, so that no radio operator could tell the world that a ship carrying Nazi diplomats was being sunk by a German sub.

As always in the navy on active service, action would be preceded by a long and tedious wait. Crowe had learned to wait—years and years of waiting had taught him how.

A bell rang at length, sharply, in the chart room behind him.

The admiral was inside on the instant, and Crowe overheard a low-voiced dialogue between him and the ensign within. Then the white uniform of the admiral showed up again, ghostly in the dark.

"They're on to something," said the admiral. "Can't get a bearing because of the ungodly noise that dressed-up hulk ahead is making. But I think your friend is in the neighborhood."

"I hope he is," said Crowe. He was not merely hardened to waiting; he was hardened to disappointment by now.

"Yes," said the admiral. Crowe was making himself stand still, and was snobbishly proud of the fact that the admiral did not seem able to do the same. Faint through the darkness Crowe could hear him humming, under his breath, "Lord Jeffrey Amherst was a soldier of the King."

Funny thing for an American admiral to be singing, Crowe told himself. Lord Jeffrey Amherst, never heard of him.

The bell rang again and yet again, and the information brought each time was more defined. Something on the port bow was moving steadily to intercept the *Wilkes*. And behind them rose the moon.

There was no chance at all of the squadron being surprised, but no one could tell just at which second the shock would come.

Somebody shouted. The gongs sounded. Crowe caught a fleeting glimpse of a long black shape breaching just off the side of the gaily lighted white hulk ahead. Then the guns broke into a roar, each report following the preceding one so closely as to make an almost continuous din. The flashes lit every part of the ship, dazzling the officers on the bridge. The destroyer was turning under full helm; not half a mile away there came a couple of answering flashes, lighting the sullen sea between. Then, as quickly as they had begun, the din and the flashes ceased. The little ship was leaping through the water now, the propeller turning at a maximum speed, now that there was no need to deceive listeners at the instruments in the submarines. The squadron was spreading out fanwise in accordance with the drill so painfully learned during preceding years. Someone shouted another order, and the depth charges began to rain into the sea.

Then the destroyers wove together again and the last depth charges searched out the areas that had escaped the teeth of the comb in the first sweep. Reports were coming up from below in a steady stream. The little ship's consorts were sending messages as well.

"We hit two," said the admiral. "I saw the bursts."

Crowe had seen them, too, but submarines have been known to survive direct hits from big shells. But if Loewenstein had been where he might have been expected to be, out watching the effect of his guns and the behavior of his subordinates, there was every chance that one of the shells had killed him.

"Only negative from down below," said the admiral.

The instruments probed the ocean depths unhampered, now that the *Wilkes* had cut her engines and was drifting. Reports said there was no trace of the solid bodies the instruments previously had contacted below the surface. Presumably, every submarine, torn open and rent asunder, had already sunk down into the freezing depths.

Crowe took the first full breath he had enjoyed since the admiral had flung his poser at him in the Navy Department office, days before. Now, he knew, the *Queen Anne* could make her run with relative security. Now he knew his hunch had been right; his hunch that Loewenstein would try to murder his helmsman, Broening.

The bell rang and some fresh information came up.

"Some indication of something on the surface. These things are too sensitive, if that's possible," said the admiral. "They tell you if a man spits overside. This'll be wreckage, I guess. . . . Listen!" he said suddenly. There was a voice hailing them from the surface. "A survivor. One of the guns' crew blown into the sea when our shells hit them."

Survivors sometimes can give even better information than wreckage. They searched carefully in the faint light of the moon to find the man who was hailing them. And when they found him and hauled him on board, Crowe recognized the pug nose and the shape of the head even through the mask of oil. It was *Korvettenkapitän* Lothar Wolfgang von und zu Loewenstein.

THE MAN WHO WAS IN LOVE WITH DEATH

LOUIS BROMFIELD

It was the music which did it—the strains of the *Intermezzo* from *Cavalleria Rusticana* played drearily by a tubercular, sallow-faced young man, an elderly pinched woman with eyes too near together and wearing pince-nez attached to her shirtwaist by a black ribbon, and an old man who had been fat in the happy days before the war and whose skin now hung in wattles over his collar. The young man played the violoncello, the woman the violin, the once fat man played the piano.

They were hired, he knew, by the hotel without any choice in the matter. It was the order of the local gauleiter that all first-class hotels must have music. It was considered good for the morale. *Das macht freudig.* Music gave the illusion of gaiety in a conquered beaten city. For whom the show was put on he could not imagine, unless it was for the foreign correspondents who lived in the Grand Brunswick Hotel. Certainly it was, or had once been, a first-class hotel. Once it had been a brilliant hotel de luxe frequented by rich and fashionable foreigners who came for the *Festspiel* or to see the architectural glories of the ancient now ruined city.

Certainly there was nothing about the music which "made gay." The three dreary people pounded the piano and sawed on the cello and the fiddle mournfully, behind their screen of tired dusty palms. It was evident how they had been selected. The young tubercular fellow was unfit for a labor camp or to work in the munitions factories. He had not the strength to do a quarter day's work. The woman was over fifty. From her appearance she had perhaps been a music teacher in the days before the Germans swarmed into the country to destroy its property and its soul. The old man at the piano had possibly played in a *bierhalle* and grown fat on treats from the patrons who liked his music. But those days were passed. There were very few patrons in *bierhallen* nowadays and the beer they drank was so weak it would make no one fat. And so the skin of the old man who was almost thin now, hung in yellow folds. Naked, he would be frightening—a picture of "famine overtakes the Pilsner drinker."

And so the three of them, ordered by the gauleiter to practice the art which once all of them had respected and loved, sawed and pounded drearily away at the music of Mascagni's *Intermezzo*. There was not enough of rebellion and bitterness in their souls to make them play badly, with deliberation. There was only the despair of people whose lives were wrecked, who were too near to death to care about anything any longer beyond a crust of bread and a cup of ersatz coffee.

"Music," he thought idly as he watched them, "might be

written or played by unhappy people but never by people in despair."

It was like the Germans to believe the mere presence of these three dreary figures making mournful sounds would deceive the correspondents into believing the city was still prosperous and gay. The Germans always had theories and plans for everything, regardless of the spirit or of the realities. It was one of the reasons why always, sooner or later, they failed. He wished for a second that he had the talent of Raemaekers to sketch in bitter lines the picture of the musicians. He would call it, "The gauleiter says that music makes gaiety."

Although he had never seen them before, he knew them the moment they began playing the *Intermezzo*. They had been with him for a long time, always in the back of his consciousness, like people he had encountered in another life. It had needed only the music to make him look up from his newspaper and notice them, sitting there behind their screen of dusty palms against the stained glass of the window depicting the Triumph of Bacchus. He knew exactly how they would look. He knew the palms and the design of the atrocious window. The whole lobby of the hotel, he saw suddenly, was exactly as he knew it would be, with its elderly clerk behind the desk, two German officers writing letters, and the fat old woman knitting in the wicker chair by the door. It was exactly as he had seen it, with the broken chairs and the patches on the ceiling where the gilt had come off. He had not been in the hotel since before Austria had been invaded, since the days when the same lobby was filled with bankers and musicians and titled people and kept women returning from the *Festspiel*.

He had never seen it like this, yet the moment the orchestra began to play, he knew it at once. He had been here before and lived through this whole scene. He had come here because, as he felt the net slowly closing in, he knew that the Grand Brunswick Hotel would be the last place they would look for him. The Grand Brunswick would be the last place they would look for a British agent whom they had trapped at last. They would be searching all the buildings in the quarter and all the other hotels, but they would scarcely look in upon the headquarters of the gestapo itself to find him. He had come in here to get his breath, to think out what must be done in order to escape. Boldness like this had turned the trick before and gotten him out of a tight place at the last moment. And so he had sat there in his black shirt and military belt, looking completely and thoroughly German, wearily trying to think of what to do before the moment arrived when they came in and recognized him and began the awful questioning.

But with the first strains of the *Intermezzo* he looked up from his newspaper and saw the orchestra and then the clerk behind the desk and the two German officers writing home and the old woman sitting in the cracked wicker chair by the door and he knew it was all up. There wasn't any use going on planning. It was all finished. In a little while Zosha would come in off the snowy street and walk past the old woman and go to the desk and ask the clerk something. Then she would come over to the one empty desk, and on her way she would pass close to him and accidentally trip over his foot. Then she would look at him without any sign of recognition and say, *"Bitte entschuldigen Sie mich! Ich muss an den Bahnhof gehen."* Then she would look at the writing desk, and as if she had changed her mind suddenly, she would turn and go out the door again into the snowy street. And in a little while he would follow her and at the corner she would be waiting, like a prostitute, and as he came up to her she would take his arm and they would walk toward the Central Railroad Station.

But beyond that he could not see. The whole thing dissolved in a kind of mist with the silhouette of the Central *Bahnhof* fading out last like a building in the fade-out at the end of a cinema. But beyond, somewhere in that mist, was capture and death. It would be a triumph for the gestapo, that at last they had run to earth and captured Eric North alias Heinrich Hostaetter alias Emile van der Hoeven alias almost anything you liked, the most dangerous man in the service. Maybe a day or two and then a wall, a volley and blackness, oblivion—and rest!

It was an odd thought that death should be as young and pretty as Zosha and as sweet and gentle. It was odd that at last, he, the cleverest of them all, should have been caught by the oldest, the most melodramatic trick of them all, by a pretty counterspy. Once or twice lately he had been suspicious. Once or twice in moments of clarity, when the weariness abated a little, he had told himself, "I must go away tonight and lose myself and never see her again." But he had fallen in love, something which had never happened to him before, something he had hoped would never happen because it rendered a man useless as a good spy. And so he had not heeded the warnings of the brain but gone on and on until now it was too late.

For he knew the truth the moment the drab little orchestra began to play. Zosha was in the counterespionage. She would come in the door presently and when she went away again he would follow her and outside somewhere in the darkness between the Hotel and the Central *Bahnhof* two or three men would come up behind them and pinion his arms and take him away. . . .

But because he was so tired and because he was in love with her, he could not even feel any resentment or bitterness. He had been a fool, as big a fool as any novice. It would bring great credit to her if she delivered him up. He did not care. Let her have the credit. He was tired, so tired that he wanted to help her and then be done with the

whole thing and rest . . . but it was odd that death should
look as young and fresh and beautiful as Zosha.

While he waited, listening idly to the despairing music,
he thought of many things, as he supposed men did who
knew they had only a few hours to live. The thoughts came
to him out of a paralyzing haze. He was unable to move or
act, and curiously he had no desire to move or act. He only
wanted peace and rest and freedom from the necessity of
planning and plotting. It would be good to die and have
done with it all, now that he knew that death looked like
Zosha. You would never again want to kiss her or hold her
in your arms, knowing that underneath that lovely face
there was only an empty skull. Love, desire, had already
been killed. Physical death was only a little way beyond.

He knew now that he should have quit and made his way
toward the border and escaped that time at Innsbruck when
he felt the first sign of weariness. It was an old story. Always
sooner or later it happened to men like himself. That awful
paralyzing weariness overtook them. It was like a disease
which destroyed their alertness, dulled their brains, and
made them useless. The service knew its danger from long
experience. The orders were to return home at the first sign
of it for a holiday or a rest, because when the weariness
came on you, you were no longer of any use. Sooner or later
you were caught and shot, or worse you were tortured and
in the weariness your own brain betrayed you and you told
them things which cost the lives of other men. That was the
only thing which troubled him now as he sat waiting for her
to come in the door. He might be so tired that when they
tortured and questioned him he would no longer know what
he was answering.

It could be very exhausting always hiding away, always
tricking those who followed you, never really sleeping at all,
always playing a role.

It was worse for him, too, because he had this awful gift of second sight, the very gift which had made him more valuable than any other man in the service. It was, he knew, a thing of nerves, of supersensitivity which made vast drains upon the vitality and health. And it was a terrifying thing, this foreknowledge of what was to come, this recognition of people you had never seen before.

No, he knew now that on the night he had collapsed in the little inn at Innsbruck, he should have fled as soon as he was strong enough, straight for the border. Or again in Vienna the time when he forgot which name he was using and what name was on his passport. They had very nearly caught him that time. Either the blond lieutenant was stupid or a little drunk or he had hated the Nazis and let him go, knowing who and what he was. He knew now that if it had been in the books for him to have been captured then, he would have known it despite his weariness. He would have seen it all just as he had seen it all now when the dreary music pulled everything together. No, it was not in the books on that occasion.

He was aware presently that the band had stopped playing. Then after a moment in which the thin old woman with the pince-nez shuffled some sheets of music about, they began again to play, this time the ballet music of *Coppélia*. That was right! That was exactly as he knew it would be! He would go to his death to the music of the doll ballet *Coppélia*.

Then the old woman rose from the wicker chair by the door and crossed to the desk. She said something to the clerk who took out some letters from a pigeonhole, looked through them and shook his head. The old woman waddled back to her chair and began knitting again. One of the young officers left the writing desk and went to the clerk's desk and bought two stamps. All that was as he knew it would be. He had forgotten that part, perhaps because some portion of his brain was numb with weariness. But it was right, exactly right! That was how it happened. And now the door would open and. . . .

The street door opened and Zosha came in out of the snowy street. She looked very young and very pretty in her blue Youth Uniform, her cheeks pink with cold, her blue eyes shining. That is the way his nibs said all Aryan German girls should look, only of course they rarely looked like that. Zosha was part Russian by blood, so she told him, but of course knowing now that Zosha was death and deception, you couldn't believe anything about her. There were snow-flakes on the shoulders of her blue uniform. The sight of her freshness and beauty roused a sudden pang, even through the mist of weariness, the last pang, perhaps.

The young officer smiled at her as he turned away from the desk, and she smiled back at him, that smile that some-times passed between young people of opposite sexes in Germany, a kind of dedicated unnatural hysterical smile, denatured and free of any sex feeling. It was no more than a sign of recognition between two individuals dedicated to the cause of *Der Führer*.

He had seen it happen before many times. It had even protected him . . . being seen with her, so young and ra-diant in her Youth Uniform. Only it was different this time. Always before it had been a deception. She had deceived the very people who said looking at her, "See! There is the ideal German girl working for the *Führer* and the new order in the world."

Only this time it was real. It was true, that friendly, in-spired smile. He thought dully, "This time the laugh is on me!" Yet he felt no bitterness.

Then she left the desk and came toward him and as she passed she tripped over his extended foot and said, *"Bitte, entschuldigen Sie mich! Ich muss an den Bahnhof gehen."* Looking up he smiled at her.

(Yes, that was right. A little comedy played against the music of *Coppélia*.)

Then she went to the writing desk and quickly turned away as if she had changed her mind. He watched her, fascinated by the fidelity of the vision he had had. But as she turned away something happened which he had not seen. She looked at him swiftly and smiled as she had smiled at the soldier, the same open, friendly, sexless smile. It was swift as a flash of heat lightning and the sight of it made him suddenly feel sick in the pit of his stomach. It was, he thought, the smile of a female Judas.

Then quickly, exactly as he had seen it, she went out of the door again and into the snowy street, and in a little while he rose and followed her, not quite knowing what he was doing, but dimly aware that whatever happened, it was better for her to have the credit of his capture than simply to sit there waiting dully until they came and arrested him. It could only be the matter of a few minutes in any case, and by now the whole thing was beyond his choice or will. He was little more than an automaton.

The feel of the cold air was like a slap in the face and for one brief moment he thought, "I could destroy the pattern. Instead of turning toward the railway station I could turn and run in the opposite direction." But he knew that he would not get far because they were searching all the district for him. It was safe to go with her. As long as he was with her, he would be free. No one would stop him or question him so long as he was in her company—until she gave the sign.

The lethargy swept over him again and, like a man hypnotized, he turned to follow her. Dimly he could see her trim figure ahead of him a little way. They were alone in the street. No other person was in sight. The police had given orders for everyone in the quarter to remain in their houses, all because they had trapped somewhere in the district a

famous spy, Eric North alias Emile van der Hoeven alias
what you will—who was himself.

"Important I am!" he thought grimly.

Then at the next corner she stopped as he knew she
would stop and waited, and as he passed, she put her arm
through his, just as she had always done when they had met
before as lovers. Neither of them spoke but she swung into
step beside him. Before them at the end of the street, silhouetted against the light of the stars, loomed the mass of
the Central *Bahnhof*. From here on he did not know what
was to happen, for the vision which came into being with
the first bars of *Cavalleria Rusticana* had gone only this far.
Beyond here lay darkness. He thought, "Perhaps I am already dead. Perhaps it is better that way." But against his
heart he felt now the warmth of her arm penetrating
through the cloth of his coat, and bitterly he thought, "The
body of a pretty woman has warmth whether or not she is a
Judas."

It had begun a long time ago, exactly when he could not
remember save that even as a small child it had happened
to him in occasional flashes, but he was too small then to
understand what it was. The first time it had happened
clearly he was fifteen years old and home in England on a
visit from Hamburg where his English father had a small
exporting business. He had arrived in a house in Surrey
which his grandmother had taken for the summer. It was a
small house with a garden, set back from the road in a small
grove of trees and approached by a winding drive. He had
never been in the house or even in Surrey in all his life, but
as the car turned in from the road, he knew it all very well,
not only the drive itself, but the house which still remained
hidden among the trees.

He saw not only the façade of the house with its flower
boxes and old-fashioned Gothic gables but his grand-

mother herself whom he had not seen for six years. The odd
part was that she appeared not as he had seen her last but
much older and thin and quite feeble. He saw her coming
down the short flight of steps to greet him, her face pink
with excitement, her hands trembling. Then the car came
round the corner of the lodge and there she was standing
in the doorway exactly as he had seen her in the moment of
clairvoyance. She had changed and aged and there was
something indefinitely feeble about her—exactly as he had
seen her during the sudden vision.

That night the vicar and his wife came to dinner and
presently while they were sitting in the drawing room, his
grandmother had asked the vicar's wife to play something
for them and the vicar's wife had gone to the piano and
played a Chopin waltz and then *Für Elise*. It was during the
Beethoven piece that it happened a second time.

It was morning and he was in this same room but there
was no one in it but himself. He was waiting for his grandmother to come to breakfast and idly watching a chaffinch
in the cherry tree outside the window when he heard a
voice behind him saying, "Excuse me for troubling you,
sir" and when he turned he saw his grandmother's old servant, his face very white, standing in the doorway. "I
would be grateful," he said, "if you would come with me. I
think something has happened to your grandmother." And
they went upstairs to his grandmother's room and there she
was quite dead in her bed.

The vicar's wife finished playing *Für Elise* and presently
she and the vicar said good night and went home and he
and his grandmother had a glass of milk each and she went
with him to his room to see that he was comfortable. When
she had gone away, he went to bed and read a mystery story
until very late, and forgot all about the curious vision he
had had while the vicar's wife was playing *Für Elise*. In
the morning he wakened and went downstairs to the draw-

ing room and was standing at the window watching a chaffinch in the cherry tree when a voice inside him said, "It is
going to happen. You must call a doctor before she dies."
But before he had time to turn he heard the voice of the old
servant saying, "Excuse me for troubling you, sir," and he
knew that it was too late. It all happened exactly as he knew
it would happen.

He said nothing of the experience to anyone, not even his
father when he arrived for the funeral, because to his sensitive adolescent mind there was something peculiar and almost indecent about the whole episode. And afterward he
could not himself be quite certain of the order in which the
experience had happened. It was as if the time element had
become muddled and confused. From time to time similar
experiences occurred—small, detached flashes, without
particular meaning. He would enter a shop and recognize
all the strangers in it—people he had never seen before, or
sometimes in the twilight border line between sleep and
wakefulness, there would occur a sudden vision of a place
which he had never seen before and of people whom he
had not yet seen.

More often than not these sudden flashes of clairvoyance
were forgotten, but sometimes the memories of them lingered, very clear and precise, so that he found himself
waiting for the pictures to become reality. Sometimes this
happened almost at once, the next day, or within a week;
but with other strange pictures, like the one in the Grand
Brunswick Hotel, they did not seem to arrive at realization
at once but slowly to fade into the mists of forgetfulness until one day perhaps months, perhaps years afterward, a
strain of music or the sight of some unfamiliar yet familiar
object would bring them to life. In the very midst of some
scene or action, he would wake suddenly to the consciousness he had known all this before and forgotten it all.

As he grew out of adolescence the experiences became

less confused and more and more sharp in detail and outline. The tormenting thing was that he seemed to have no control whatever over the visions; they occurred without reason or logical succession. Once or twice he thought, "If only I could control this peculiar gift, I could conquer the whole world. I could win all bets at the races. I could make fortunes at investments." But there was no way to control these flashes of foreknowledge.

Once when he was eighteen and home in Hamburg from Oxford, he spoke of the experience to his father while they were walking through the fields on Sunday afternoon. But his father, an unimaginative, materialistic man, had only laughed at him and said that all people had such experiences from time to time, especially that of entering a strange room and feeling they had been there before. It was nothing remarkable, he said. If it had been remarkable, he pointed out, some practical use would have been made of the gift long ago.

So he never again mentioned it to his father, not troubling to point out that doubtless only people of an imaginative, sensitive, and impractical nature were endowed with the gift.

But it troubled him, crippling and deforming all the ordinary relationships of life. How was it possible to embark upon a friendship with a man when suddenly without warning you knew how it was to end, in a betrayal of confidence or a bitter quarrel. How was it possible to marry or take a mistress with that awful power of foreknowledge perpetually making the relationship impossible. It made him shy with people and rather solitary by nature. All his nattural sensitiveness became sharpened to a point where at times life grew almost unbearable. But worst of all was the confusion it produced in the element of time. There were occasions when it seemed to him that he lived simultaneously in the past, the present, and the future, when his brain seemed divided into three parts, each dominated by a different place in time, operating without coordination. It was exhausting, and when he was twenty-six the world seemed to collapse all about him and he had a breakdown and was sent to a remote village in the Tyrol to recover.

Here he met the scientist who made it possible for him to regain control of himself, to order his existence once more, and to prevent the strange gift from ruining all his life.

The man was thin and tall and over fifty and had spent all his life in surgery and physiology. He knew more than any other living man concerning the human body, its muscles, its bones, its nerves, its organs. He knew so much that he had become aware of having reached the limits of the physical. There was, he believed, nothing more to be learned from operations and dissections; one had to go beyond into the realm which science had always overlooked and neglected—that realm of the mystical in which occurred such things as clairvoyance and thought transference and that strange thing the time element which had perpetually deceived mankind, and distorted all conscious existence. His attitude was entirely scientific, and he had come to the point where all the mechanistic and physiological achievements of his celebrated past no longer interested him. He stood at the threshold of a limitless world, veiled in mists into which few scientists had ever looked.

The surgeon had come to the Tyrolean village to lose himself intellectually, to sever if possible all relationship with the material world of his past achievement. No one knew he was there. No one could find him. In this mood, at breakfast one morning, he came upon the young Englishman who had the strange gift.

That the young man was ill was apparent to him at once, and that the illness was not of the body but of the sensitivity he discovered before very long. The illness affected the body only in so far as the strain upon it wearied the tissues and the organs. The illness came not of the body but from outside it. After a day or two as they walked and ate together it became apparent to him that the illness was born of what might be described as maladjustment between the body and the superacuteness of the young man's perceptions. In their conversations he discovered that the young fellow frequently knew the end of a sentence the surgeon himself was speaking—sometimes even a complicated sentence requiring thought—before he had reached the end. He himself had something of the gift, and so after a week he found that they were conversing and even exchanging ideas almost without speaking, certainly never in rounded completed sentences. To the scientist and surgeon, it was as if God had sent him a subject to work upon.

Then one night while they were sitting in the taproom of the village inn, smoking their pipes and drinking beer, the young Englishman said, "The girl is going to sing a song called *Ein Kleines Hotel* and she will sing it to the young man over there by the window and when she has finished singing it, Fritz, the guide, will get up and go over to her and slap her face."

He did not know why he said it except that saying it brought a relief to his nerves and because the personality of the scientist seemed to make it possible. He could not have said it to anyone else in the world.

The scientist did not reply. He relighted his pipe and as he did so the girl took up her accordion and after a flash of notes, began to sing. The song was *Ein Kleines Hotel*. She looked directly at the young man sitting by the window and when it was finished, Fritz, the guide, rose, crossed the room, and slapped her face. It all happened exactly as Eric had seen it.

When Fritz had been thrown out and the uproar died down, the doctor asked, "How did you know that?"

"I don't know. I saw it quite clearly."

"Did you see anything beyond that?"

"Nothing. After the slap the whole thing faded into a mist."

After that it was easier to talk, and he told the scientist more and more of what had happened to him since that first experience with the death of his grandmother. And the more he talked the easier it became to talk, and the tension of his nerves slackened and health began to return.

There were many things which interested the older man —that there was no way of knowing when the flashes of foreknowledge were to happen, that there was no way of knowing at what point they would halt. Sometimes they seemed to carry on to an end, like a complete and isolated incident. At others they went only so far and then seemed to dissolve in the wall of fog.

The scientist explained about the time element and the lag between an actual occurrence and the brain's recording of it—that the incident in the taproom might only have been evidence of the boy's supersensitivity, that what he had experienced was not foreknowledge but only came from the possibility that one part of the boy's brain reacted much more quickly than another part of it.

The older man was not only brilliant, he was kind. He tried to help the young man while using him as a laboratory specimen.

"You must accept these experiences as a kind of special endowment," the older man told him. "You must accept them as simple ordinary facts. It would be best to control them if you can find any way of doing so. It would be a good idea to attempt turning them to advantage. In any case you must not again allow the experience to hypnotize and paralyze you."

"How can I help it if always they turn out to be true?"

For that there was no answer save only the weak one the scientist gave. "Perhaps one day it will happen that you see wrongly—that the thing does not happen as you saw it."

Then one morning the scientist received a telegram and left. As he said good-by, he added, "We must not lose each other. I will come back or you must come to see me in America. The rest of my life I am giving to finding out what I can about such things."

They planned to meet in a few months' time and they would have met but for forces far more powerful than either of them. The young man had a telegram calling him back to London and when he arrived, his uncle met him at Victoria Station. His uncle was in the Foreign Office and at lunch in his flat he told the young man that there was a job he could do to help his country. He knew Germany and especially Hamburg and Berlin. He spoke German like a German and French very nearly as well. He could pass as a German or a Belgian. There were some things in Germany which the government wished to discover.

The young man thought it over for twenty-four hours. It seemed a wise thing to do. It might help him back on his feet. He might find in such a task some practical use for his extraordinary gift which would make it bearable and even useful.

And so he became a secret agent, the most remarkable one in the whole of Germany, because again and again, there occurred to him moments of clairvoyance which saved his life, or provided him with an extraordinary piece of information, or enabled him to discover and betray a counterspy. But at last they tracked him down, into a block of buildings between the Grand Brunswick Hotel, and the Central *Bahnhof*, because he was tired, because even the strong, healthy body nature had given him could no longer endure the strain of his frightening gift.

And now here he was walking along the dark street toward the railway station and his death with indifference, al-

most happily because he could feel the warmth of her body
against his arm. For the moment it didn't matter whither
she led him as long as her youth and strength were there
near to him. Once long ago when he had gone away to the
Tyrol, he had been like this, dull and numb and indifferent
to everything save the solace and relief of sleep which was
next to death. It was like that now. Then he was aware
suddenly that they had passed that point in the vision
where it faded into mist with only the silhouetted mass of
the railway station black against the night sky.

They were still walking and out of the doorways no men
had yet come to step behind him and pinion his arms and
say, "*Herr* North-van der Hoeven!" but he remembered that
he had not seen the men; that part he had only imagined, so
there was no inevitability about it. That did not *have* to
happen. She might herself lead him directly to the Central
Police Station.

She did not speak save once when she said in her faintly
accented English, "Are you tired?" and he answered, "Yes,
very tired."

They were walking very close to the buildings now, those
great blank walls of Central European apartment houses
which even in peacetime had an air of gloom about them,
and suddenly by a gentle pressure she turned him and
thrust him into a darkened doorway. It was not, he saw, the
main entrance of the great building but a small door. Free-
ing his arm she took a key from a pocket in her trim blue uniform, thrust it into the lock, and opened the door. Quickly
they went through it into the darkness beyond. She locked
it behind them and then said, "There are stairs. Be careful!"

Again with her arm through his, she led him down iron
stairs until their feet struck a floor of concrete. He kept
thinking, "It will come to me now at any second and I will
know where I am and what is to happen." But he saw no

more in his mind than he saw with his eyes. No clue came, no hint, no clear forewarning such as he had had swiftly at the first notes of the *Intermezzo*.

Then she said, "Stairs again!" and they climbed another flight of iron stairs which rang beneath their feet and came after a little time onto a floor of tiles. She appeared to know her way well in the darkness for she did not falter nor grope with her hand along the wall. Then she unlocked another door and they went into a room. Here she withdrew her arm again, this time to strike a match and light a candle. The tiny flame illumined her face and he felt a sudden glow of feeling that was like a strain of music, like the swelling bell music out of *Boris Godunov*. For a second he knew again what was to happen.

She would take the candle and place it inside the door of a cupboard built into the wall and then close the door a little way so that the flame did not shine directly into the room. Then she would return and say, "Lie down on the divan. You must be very tired."

It happened like that, exactly, but the vision went no further. The mist closed down again. He thought, "I am tired. That is why." But there was too the fact that one part of his spirit was stubbornly unwilling to see any further. It would not be possible to endure knowing exactly how the betrayal would happen. It would be unbearable. His body made him want to deny the vision in the Grand Brunswick lobby. His body, because it loved her, wanted him to go on being deceived until the very last second.

Then she sat down beside him on the edge of the sofa and began to stroke his forehead. Her hand was still cold with the cold of the snowy streets.

She said, "You must stay here. I must go now and you must stay here until I come for you. It would be unsafe to go outside. This room belongs to the concierge. He is a Communist. He is waiting for the Day to rise. They have already been here and searched the room. They will not come again, but outside they will be watching everywhere. Even your uniform would do you no good now."

He realized that her hand was trembling.

Then she bent down and kissed his forehead. In the darkness he thought, The kiss! That was all that was needed. Aloud he said, "Perhaps it would be easier if I went out and gave myself up."

She laughed, an odd almost inhuman laugh. "No, you mustn't do that. Fabrizius wants the credit of catching you." Then she rose and went out the door. Dimly he realized that she turned the key in the lock on the outside.

Fabrizius! That was it! Just as he had imagined. She had saved him from the local gestapo and military only to save him for Fabrizius. Fabrizius was her chief. "They" had told him that when they had given him orders to meet her on a bench in the Tiergarten in Berlin. She was officially working for Fabrizius, but that meant nothing, "they" said. She was playing the most dangerous of double games, that of informer who had worked herself high into the confidence of the gestapo. It was odd how intricately it worked, this world of double cross and double double cross which Hitler and Himmler had invented. It was odd that even when agents saw him with her he was safe, because they believed she was gaining information from him. More than once before now they might have picked him up but for her presence. He wondered for how long they had been on his trail this time. Perhaps they had followed him to Flensburg and then all the way across Germany to Munich and then here into this Czech city. Perhaps they had been with him all along only waiting for her to give the sign to arrest him. One thing was clear. There was jealousy and intrigue at work inside the organization. The local crowd had gotten wind of his presence and tried to trap him and gain all the credit. Somehow she had led him out of the lion's mouth here to this janitor's room, to save him and the credit of capturing him for her chief, the dread Fabrizius.

But in his weariness he did not care what happened to him. He opened his eyes presently and regarded the room. It was cheaply furnished with a table, a few chairs, some photographs and a large picture of Hitler with a Nazi flag draped over it. What had she meant by saying the occupant of this room was a Communist waiting for the Day to come? Did she think him a fool or did she not notice that the picture was here? But almost at once he saw his own naïveté. Of course, if the man was an undercover Communist he would have a picture of Hitler and a Nazi flag— the biggest he had room for.

It was all so complex and complicated, this world into which he and Zosha had been born. You could trust no one. In their hearts, no one in Germany trusted anyone else. That was why there was so much cruelty and fear. When you could not trust, you must dominate by evil, by force, by fear, by cruelty, however the domination might be achieved.

He remembered the day he was sent to meet her in the Tiergarten. She was, "they" said, young and blonde and beautiful. *Beautiful* was the word "they" used, not *pretty*. They said, "She is not like the usual female agent. She looks her part . . . like a young girl who is an officer in the Youth Movement. But she is clever. She is half-Russian. We have investigated. She is absolutely trustworthy. She will be of good use to you. She will be able to get you into all sorts of difficult places and out of them. Everybody trusts her. She looks like Hitler's ideal Aryan maiden. No one even suspects her."

So he had gone to the Tiergarten and there on a bench in the Siegesalle near the statue of Frederick the Great he found her. She was feeding the squirrels with crumbs of bread. (Even the poor squirrels were rationed.) He knew

that she was aware of him before he sat on the bench beside
her. Anyone watching them would have thought it was a
kind of healthy flirtation between two big blond Nordics—
between Hitler's two ideals, the big blond storm trooper
and the Aryan maiden.

They talked first about the squirrels and then about the
rather neglected condition of the park. "In wartime," she
said, "there is neither time nor money for such luxuries as
parks." And presently they allowed the casual pretense to
drift away and she said in a low voice, "Where shall we meet
again?" And he suggested a well-known restaurant in the
Kurfürstendam. There, with lights and music, they would
be able to talk. No one would suspect them. They would be
two young Nazi fiancés having a dinner of celebration together. "My name," he said, "is Heinrich Paul." And she answered, "I am Zosha Hirth. I am part Russian. I speak Russian and Polish." She added, "That makes me valuable."

Then they talked a little longer, about what he could no
longer remember, for the spell had already begun to work
and he was thinking, despite himself, that she was beautiful and had a lovely low voice. Presently she said, "I think
we had better go now." It was growing late and people returning from work were beginning to cross the park. They
stood up and she raised her arm and said, "*Heil* Hitler!" and
he did the same. Then they went off in opposite directions
to meet again at the Kurfürstendam restaurant.

But the thing had happened already.

He did not know how or why it happened but he did
know that what had happened to him had never happened
before. He had had other girls. In his work women were important. They were a part of the job, and for his age he was
far more experienced than most men. And there was always
that other thing of which most men had nothing—that curious vision which told him so much, nearly always too
much, about them on a first encounter. But the thing which

happened to him on the bench in the Tiergarten was like nothing he had ever known before. It was what was called love at first sight.

His friend the surgeon had described it to him, analyzing it with the dispassionate detachment of a scientist. It happened, he said, when two bodies suited each other, when two minds and spirits were complementary. There were in it also the elements of chemistry and of mysticism, neither of which elements science had yet dealt with adequately. "Love at first sight," he had said, "is an experience which is scientifically possible, but very rare. A great many inferior people like to deceive themselves into believing they have experienced it, but in reality very few have ever known anything like it. The Greeks, the old poets, Shakespeare understood what it was. . . . They conjured up love potions and gods and goddesses to make the experience seem reasonable, because love at first sight was even to them a superromantic and illogical experience. Nevertheless it existed and does sometimes exist. Take Tristram and Isolde. . . . There you had it. . . ."

Lying there on the janitor's cot in the darkness, he could hear the great man, disillusioned as scientists can be, but romantic as only scientists can be, talking on and on. Oddly enough the lecture had made no difference to his own emotions. It had made him neither disillusioned nor cynical. Not even the knowledge that there was no place for love in the hideous calling he practiced, that in the hideous calling love almost invariably led to betrayal and death, made any difference.

In the darkness he smiled, not without bitterness. He had believed that she too loved him. He had believed that she had arranged it so that she could be with him in Flensburg and Munich and now here. He had believed that she had protected and shielded him. And all the time she was acting on the orders of Fabrizius.

Suddenly through his thoughts came the sound of footsteps in the hallway outside the door. Someone knocked, once and then again. He sat up more out of long habit than because he was alarmed. He thought, Now they've come. They followed us here. They'll take me first before she can lead me into Fabrizius' trap.

But it was not the gestapo. They would have yelled, "Open up!" and beaten down the door. Once more the knock was repeated. Then the sound of footsteps going away.

He lay back again closing his eyes and wishing it were all over. It was odd that he felt no resentment against her. Perhaps it was because he was so tired, perhaps because he loved her so much. He thought, It's all the fault of this damnable world into which we were born, a world of hate and misery. But for all this misery about them, they might have met and loved each other and been married and had a family and lived happily. At the back of the thought lay the memory of the three dreary musicians at the Grand Brunswick Hotel, fiddling and pounding dismally at the *Intermezzo* and the ballet music. They were the proper symbols of this tired world in which he and Zosha had met —the tubercular man, the ugly old woman, the old man with the folds of yellow skin hanging over his soiled collar. How could there be normal happiness in such a world? How could there be loyalty or decency? How could there be anything but despair and betrayal? Even hope became hysterical, like the insane cheering he had seen at Nazi party meetings, like the insane fervor which made a normal healthy girl like Zosha give herself over body and soul to a vile organization like the gestapo.

I am, he thought, already dead. So what? What good is there to live in such a world?

Then presently out of sheer weariness he fell asleep. For three days and three nights he had been fleeing, watchful, aware that any man he passed on the street might be the one who would thrust a pistol into his ribs and say, *"Nun, Herr* Heinrich Paul." He dreamed that they came and broke down the door and took him and that when they went outside he found others kicking and beating an elderly man who they said was the janitor. They were kicking him to death because he was a Communist who pretended to be for Hitler. And Zosha was there, young and beautiful. She was standing by, saying, "Kick harder! Make him yell!" Only somehow, it was not Zosha but another young girl—a whole composition of young girls (the insane faces kept changing) whom he had seen screaming and yelling like mad women at party meetings.

It was dawn when he wakened, slowly, not knowing at first where he was or how he had come there. It was the large photograph of Hitler which made him remember all that had happened the night before. Slowly he went back over every incident, and now that he had slept a little it seemed to him that he had been a fool all along, from the very moment he sat on the bench beside her in the Tiergarten. He felt an odd sense of shame that he should have fallen into the oldest trap there was, and then found a little consolation in the fact that he had not been the only one deceived. "They"—the mysterious, powerful "they" who gave him orders—had believed in her too. But "they" had not been in love with her. There lay the difference.

The sleep had brought him no sense of rest and well-being because the weariness and the illness were of the spirit and the mind, an illness so great that he remained paralyzed and incapable of action. There was, he knew sitting there on the edge of the janitor's cot, nothing to do but wait. Wait for what? he asked himself and the answer came back, For death!

He considered the prospect dully and without emotion.

He had been like this before, that time in the Tyrol, when he did not care whether he lived or died. Death would mean rest, release from being hunted, release from those sudden flashes of clairvoyance which made life unendurable. If only once what he saw in the visions had been wrong, he could have endured it, but what he saw was always right. It always happened exactly as he saw it. Now he knew he was too tired for the visions to trouble him. They would not come when he was like this, numb and exhausted.

While he sat there in a kind of fog, the sound of footsteps came to him. They were her footsteps; he would have known them anywhere. Then the key turned in the lock and she came in, carrying a cheap paper suitcase in her hand.

She came over to him and stroked his forehead as she had done the night before. "Are you feeling rested?" she asked.

"Yes . . . and you? Have you slept?"

"A little. They are still watching but they are letting people go in and out now."

"What are we going to do?"

"I've a plan . . . a very old theatrical plan but it may work for that reason."

She placed the suitcase on the bed beside him, opened it, and took out a man's suit of clothes, a shirt, tie, shoes and socks, an overcoat, and a hat. "You are going to wear these," she said. "Better change into them quickly. You must go out at the hour when people are going to work. They will notice you less then."

He was aware of an odd theatrical quality about the whole scene. He might have said, "Why do you do this to me? Why trouble to deliver me to Fabrizius? Why not let the ones waiting outside take me?" But he felt an odd embarrassment. He could not ask her these things. Remembering the past and how much he loved her, he could not face the ugliness of accusing her. It was much better to let it happen the other way. It was better to go with her, letting her believe that he still trusted her. Then she would arrange it so that when he was arrested she would not be present. He would never see her again and after a little while they would shoot him and he would have rest.

It was much better that way, much better for her and for the love that had been and perhaps still was between them. It would have existed forever but for this other unnatural love of hers, this curious German devotion toward an idea. That was stronger in Germany than the love between man and woman, between mother and son. It was evil, fanatic, something he could never quite understand. In the end it would die because it was inhuman, like the fanaticism of some Communists, but before it died it would have destroyed many lives and made the whole pleasant world a wretched place.

No, he could not accuse her now. He was lost in any case, and so it seemed to him evil and needless to destroy all that had been beautiful by a moment or two of bitter ugliness. No, let her go on thinking that she had deceived him.

He began taking off his storm trooper's uniform and she said, "Give me your papers. I must have the photograph for the new passport."

As he changed into the dark suit of business clothes, he watched her working deftly on the corner of the janitor's table. She had stamps which she was transferring. She used the surface of a hard-boiled egg to transfer the inking of a rubber stamp. She worked surely and skillfully. By the time he had finished changing, she stood up, finished with her work. Handing him a passport and a wallet partly filled with money and papers, she said, "You are Swiss now. You are comptroller of a bank in Montreaux. You are here to finish up some business for the estate of a Swiss who owned property here. You have been in Montreux?"

"Yes. Many times."

"Can you imitate Swiss German?"

"Ein wenig aber nur ein bisschen." He spoke thickly. The thing had become a grim sort of joke which made him want to laugh.

"If anyone stops you," she said, "lay it on thick. I will keep your storm trooper's papers. Found on me they will mean nothing." She opened a small box. "There is one more thing. This is the funny part."

She took out a pair of spectacles and a blond false mustache. "It's silly but it may work."

With spirit gum she fastened the mustache to his lip. Then she took up the glasses. "I hope you can see through them. They are very thick, for a very nearsighted person. Dark glasses were too obvious."

He put them on and the whole room became a dark blur. The bed, the table, the portrait of *Der Führer* were barely discernible, little more than dim outlines.

"I would not know you," she said. "You are middle-class, bourgeois, solid, dull. You look like all bankers." She sighed, "It may work after all." Then she took the storm trooper's clothes under her arm. "We mustn't leave them here. If they were found it would be hard on our friend, the janitor."

That was like her, like the Zosha he loved, to think of the janitor.

"Come," she said, "it is time. Bring the suitcase. It is empty but that won't matter. If they question you it will be all over anyway."

Opening the door, she looked up and down the narrow hallway and then beckoned to him. In order to see properly, he pushed the gold-rimmed glasses high on his forehead and followed her.

She went down a narrow iron stairway into a vast cellar. They had, he knew, come this way on the night before when they had vanished out of the snowy street. Now she took him to the far end of the cellar and opening a steel door, she said, "Be careful as you can. Don't get yourself covered with coal dust and soot."

The passage was narrow and low and filled with steam pipes. In the days when there was coal, the pipes had supplied the other great apartment houses in the block with heat from a central plant in the vast cellar they had left. Halfway down the long passage she stuffed his storm trooper's uniform behind the pipes. "When they find it," she said, "they will know the bird has flown."

At the end of the passage they came into another vast cellar. Crossing this, she led him again up an iron stairway and when she opened the door at the top they were in the main hallway of an apartment house.

Behind the cage of the elevator she handed him a railway ticket. "There is your ticket to Freiburg. I will be on the train but I will not be in the same compartment. If you see me remember that you do not know me. They may suspect that I am taking the prize to Fabrizius. They may be watching me. Now go!"

She did not offer to kiss him and he thought, That is very decent of her. She could not bring herself to do it. Perhaps she is going away now. Perhaps this is the last time I shall see her. Perhaps on the way to Freiburg they will take me.

It was better like that.

But suddenly she took hold of his arm. "Are you well? Are you quite all right? Can you make it alone?"

"I'm tired. That's all. I'm quite all right."

"Good-by then."

"Good-by."

It struck him that she said "good-by" and not *"auf Wiedersehen."* As she went through the door back again into the vast cellar, he felt his heart contract with a wild pang of sorrow and bitterness for all the delight, the happiness that should have been theirs forever, but which they would never know again because they were born of an accursed

generation in an accursed world. What had been meant by
God had been shattered by the evil in man.

Then squaring his shoulders as a kind of gesture because
he knew it would take all the energy he possessed and all
the cool headedness to pass the line of guards in the street
and later at the station, he pulled the thick glasses over his
eyes, picked up the cheap suitcase and, half-blinded, made
his way toward the door.

It was simpler than he had hoped. At the end of the street
two men stopped him and demanded his papers. He could
not see their faces. The thickness of the glasses blurred
them, and he thought, Perhaps the glasses have changed
me too. It was odd the confidence the glasses gave him. It
was not only that they changed the whole world, they
seemed to change himself, blurring his personality, dull-
ing him.

"And your business?" one of them asked.

"Banker, here to settle an estate."

"You have visited the police control?"

"My passport has the stamp . . . see?"

The man asked, "That is your photograph?"

"Yes . . . without my glasses." He knew he had made a
slip there, but there was no other way out. He continued to
speak with what he hoped was a thick Swiss accent.

"Take off your glasses."

He took off the glasses, blinking and peering realistically
and was relieved to see that he had never seen either agent
before. Sooner or later he came to recognize those who followed him. The man who questioned him had a rat's face,
like Goebbels. It was astonishing how many of them had
that rodent look, like weasels.

"And the mustache . . . does it come off too?"

"Bitte . . . ." he said stupidly.

It was a bad moment.

"What were you doing here in this block?" the man asked.

"I spent the night with my cousin Herr Luckenback. He lives in the flat at Number 33."

"*Parlez-vous francais?*"

"*Naturellement. Je viens de Montreux.*"

That seemed to do it. Why, he was never quite certain. The man gave him back the passport. He put down the suitcase and readjusted his glasses. He took his time about it. He must save himself for Fabrizius so that she would get the credit of having captured the prize.

The man with the weasel face said, "Another banker pig!" Then they turned and left him suddenly before he had adjusted the glasses again and picked up the suitcase. He was deliberate and slow.

Not until he reached the railway station did he feel safe once more. It was all right he knew now unless he met some agent who had actually seen him before and might recognize him. The glasses made him dizzy and produced an awful aching in the top of his head.

At the railway station there appeared to be quite a crowd leaving. The police control seemed to discover nothing suspicious. The fat lieutenant only asked, "Your business here?"

"To settle an estate."

"Finished?"

"*Gut.*" He snapped the passport shut and returned it but the word *finished* echoed after he had gone through the gateway. Finished, that was it. Even if he had had a desire to escape, he was finished. He would never again be any good. It was easier to heal a terrible wound than to heal shattered nerves. But he felt a kind of odd perverse pleasure at having tricked them thus far. Perhaps it was only habit, the long habit of the satisfaction the hunted felt in outwitting the hunter.

The weariness came over him again, a strange numbness which seemed to paralyze all his actions. On the train he found himself a place in a second-class compartment, and almost at once he closed his eyes. He dared not take off his glasses and the lenses tortured him, aggravating the sharp pain in the top of his head. Suddenly he felt consciousness slipping from him. It was not sleep. He was fainting. The blurred world about him whirled and faded into mistiness.

When he wakened he was aware, slowly at first, of the sunlight coming in at the window on the opposite side of the room. It was a room he had never seen before but he knew it at once by the pattern of light on the ceiling. It was sunlight reflected from water and it danced in a crazy pattern which at first hurt his eyes. Then slowly he knew what he would find in the room. Opposite him there would be a carved heavy wooden cupboard with figures of elves and gnomes dancing across the top, and there would be a table with a white lace cloth and an aspidistra and a red carpet and two small chairs and a heavy deep Victorian chair upholstered in red plush, and in it she would be sitting occupied with some sort of needlework . . . knitting it was. He did not know in what town the room existed nor what had happened before or what was to come afterward. The room, as he saw it, was simply there isolated in time and space.

"Perhaps," he thought, "I am already dead."

The most remarkable thing was her presence in the room. She had said good-by—not *"auf Wiedersehn"* but "good-by"—there in the black hallway of the apartment house and gone away forever, closing the door. She had gone away forever, leaving Fabrizius' gang to pick him up on the train.

But if he were not dead, it was clear that they had not arrested him for this room was not a prison cell. Before he could summon his courage to look away from the sun-speckled white ceiling, he tried desperately to remember what had happened after he went aboard the train. But he could remember only as far as the compartment. What had happened after that, how he came into this room, he did not know. In his brain there seemed to be only a swirling mist out of which faces emerged from time to time, faces of strangers mostly but once or twice her face appeared vaguely for a moment or two.

He thought, "I must have been very ill. Now I must look at this room."

He turned his head and there it was exactly as he had seen it and she was sitting there in the big old-fashioned plush chair, knitting, turned so that he saw her profile against the bright sunlight. Only she was not wearing the familiar blue uniform. She was dressed in a cheap, rather ill-fitting jacket and skirt. There was something dowdy and domestic about the scene, as if they had been happily married for a long time, so happily married that she had ceased even to care about her appearance.

He waited, watching her for a long time, aware of a vast inward comfort and happiness, afraid to speak lest he would shatter it only to discover that the whole thing had no reality. But at last, summoning his courage, he said, "Zosha." His voice sounded weak and strange, but it was strong enough to rouse her. She turned toward him and said quickly, "Eric! Are you all right, my sweetheart?"

She rose quickly out of the chair and came over to the bed. Beyond her through the window he saw painted high on the building opposite, *Zuricher Bäckerei*, Zurich Bakery. Zurich was in Switzerland. Zurich!

"I'm all right, I think," he said. "Why are you here?"

"I brought you here. We are in Switzerland. You are safe now, my darling. Never again must you go back into that poor, accursed country."

"Tell me . . . you said 'good-by.' You went away."

She began stroking his forehead with the old gesture. She

who was so calm had discovered long ago the relief it brought his nerves.

"Don't try to talk now," she said. "Listen to me. I will tell you everything."

"My darling," he said. And he was thinking, What I saw in the Grand Brunswick Hotel was not true. For once I saw a lie. Now I am free.

"You must be very quiet," she said. He was aware that she had changed in some subtle way. Not only had her appearance changed but her very voice seemed different. She was talking now, telling him what had happened and how they came to be here in this shabby room in Zurich, safe and together.

She told it simply, as quickly as she could, and as he listened the wonder and love in his heart swelled until it seemed to him that it would burst.

She had, she said, got aboard the train in a suburb of the city and by some good chance she chose the coach in which he was traveling. Inside the coach she found excitement because a man traveling in a second-class compartment had fainted. When she discovered that it was her Swiss banker, she said, "I am a nurse, I will take charge."

She was afraid of many things—that there might be a gestapo agent on the train, that some stranger might go through the pitifully inadequate papers with which she had stuffed his wallet, that the absurd mustache might come off. When the train started moving again, she made the most of the situation, asking the other passengers to leave the compartment so that the sick man might have quiet. Closing the door and drawing the curtains she placed a pillow beneath his head and sat with him. Now and then, she said, he had recovered consciousness and talked for a little while although of this he himself remembered nothing.

Sitting there beside him she had plotted desperately,

working out plot after plot only to reject each one because
of some flaw in it. It was impossible of course to take him to
any hospital because the police would come in at once and
begin asking questions. As far as Freiburg there would possibly be little difficulty. She could go on in her uniform pretending she was a nurse. So long as he slept or was uncon-
scious, they would probably leave him in peace. If any of
Fabrizius' men were about they would not trouble him,
believing all the time that she was taking him to Munich by
a roundabout way to deceive the other faction. But from
Freiburg on, when they took a train for the border instead
of for Munich, there would be trouble at once.

So, after a long time, she decided that there was but one
course to take, a bold one. It was to play upon his illness, to
exploit it; but in order to do this she would herself have to
find a new role, and at last she settled upon what it was to
be. In Freiburg she would have to buy clothes, dowdy Swiss
clothes, throw away her neat blue uniform, and become his
sister. She had her own forged passport, prepared like his
own, by one of Fabrizius' own men. They were both tall,
blond, and blue-eyed. It was easy to mistake them for
brother and sister. She would be his sister who had come
from Switzerland to take him home. She invented a whole
story, down to the most minute details, a whole family history with marriages and divorces to explain the difference
in the names on their passports. So long as he remained in a
dazed and incoherent state, there would be no danger of his
being questioned. They could not discover from his an-
swers that she was lying.

On the train no one troubled them. Twice the conductor
and once a policeman opened the compartment door to ask
after the sick man. Each time they had gone away she had
sat up stiffly and said, "*Heil* Hitler!" If they had had any sus-
picions—and in Germany there were few people and no

officials who did not have them—they were allayed at once by the picture of the blonde Nordic girl in party uniform, raising her hand in the party salute.

At Freiburg she managed to rouse him sufficiently to get him to his feet and recruited the aid of the ticket comptroller to get him off the train, through the gate, and into the station. Anyone seeing them could not doubt the genuineness of the sick man's condition. The girl and the ticket comptroller were forced to support him between them. People stared at them but now in the stares there was no suspicion but only curiosity and sometimes sympathy.

In the big waiting room she found a porter, a kindly old man, and paid him to keep watch over the sick man while she went into the town to do some business. She took the cheap suitcase with her and in a department store she purchased a shoddy suit, a hat, and a blouse. Putting these into the suitcase she went to a public lavatory and there changed from her uniform into the new clothes.

"It was an extraordinary feeling," she said. "It was as if I had become a new and different woman. Whatever remained of the old life seemed to be washed away. It gave me fresh courage. I was sure then that the plan I had worked out would go through, unless one of Fabrizius' men was still following us. If he saw me buying tickets for Zurich or saw us get on the Swiss train, then we were lost."

He listened to her story in a kind of daze, confused and puzzled, and only clearly aware of the fact that she was sitting there on the bed beside him, her hand in his. That to him was all that mattered. He was aware vaguely that what she was telling him was an heroic story, because at each stop she risked torture and death, but the elements and motives in it were still confused in the weariness of his brain. When he looked at her, he was aware again of the great change in her. She was no longer a young girl, but a woman. She was older and more subdued but also more tender. This

too puzzled him, for although the rescue and escape was
in itself a nerve-racking experience, it was not enough to
have changed her so profoundly.

Suddenly she bent down and kissed him and he felt her
tears on his cheeks. Then she sat up very straight again and
went on with the story.

When she returned to the station she found him still sitting on the bench where she had left him, awake now but
staring in front of him into space. The old porter looked at
her and remarked that she had changed her clothes.

"Yes," she told him, "I am crossing the border on a mis-
sion. Our uniform is not welcome on the other side of the
border."

"Perhaps one day," said the old man.

"Perhaps one day," she echoed. "*Heil* Hitler!"

"*Heil* Hitler!" said the old man.

Then she bought the tickets, studying the people about
her and those waiting in the station. She could discover no
one who seemed to be one of Fabrizius' agents, no one certainly she had ever seen before. Smiling to herself, she
thought, He must have trusted me to have let me go un-
watched. It was rare that he did not have an agent en-
gaged upon important business shadowed by another agent.

Luckily there had been little time between trains, barely
enough for her to hurry into the town and effect the change
in her appearance. Now with the aid of the old porter she
managed to get him through the gate, past all the officials
and safely onto the train. Neither the police nor the railway
officials made much show of inspecting their papers, again
perhaps because they both appeared to be so blond and
such splendid specimens of the race which the small, dark
Goebbels extolled. But there was another element which
protected them, the potent fact of his collapse and nearness
to death. It had blotted out all else. People had gathered
about them curiously, the way she had seen cattle in a field

gather about a sick and dying animal, the way cattle gathered about the spot where an animal had been slaugh-
tered.

When the stationmaster had remarked, "The young man
is ill. You had better take him to a hospital," she had said,
"Yes, utter collapse. The doctors said the only chance of
saving him was to take him home at once."

"He was a flier?" the man asked with sympathy.

"Yes . . . a flier. A Stuka."

"Ach . . . that is bad. And so young too."

Then he had helped them, the traitress and the spy, into
the train and himself fetched a pillow to place beneath the
head of the sick man.

The fact of his illness blotted out all else, perhaps because it brought madness and death painfully near to all
those who stood like cattle in a field, watching. It occurred
to her that if the illness had been faked, the effect would
have been lost. The very illness had a power of its own. It
was as if it surrounded them in its own protective aura.

The rest of the story was simple and brief. In the night
she had thrown her party uniform out of the window somewhere between Freiburg and the border, and at the frontier
there was little trouble. It was four in the morning, the hour
when death comes to the ill and unwary. The officials tried
to rouse the sick man to ask him one or two questions but it
was clear that he was beyond the possibility of being
roused to consciousness and after a little while, sympa-
thetically, they went away.

As the train pulled over the frontier into Switzerland she
began to cry. She wept uncontrollably for a long time until
she thought of Fabrizius in his office in Munich when the
news came that not only the most famous foreign secret
agent in Germany had again escaped but that one of his
own agents had disappeared with him. Fabrizius would

scream in his high-pitched voice and smash with his riding whip anything breakable in his office. And then—she shuddered at this—he would go down to the prison and wreak his sadistic vengeance on the helpless prisoners. And presently she began to cry again, all her courage and daring melted and collapsed now. She wept for the prisoners of her beloved lacerated Germany, for herself, for what she had believed, because for a little time she had come very near to committing the greatest crime a woman can commit.

When she had finished she kissed him again and said, "But we are not free yet. The police here will come and question us about our papers."

He scarcely heard her for what happened to them now did not trouble him. They were over the border out of that monstrous country of suspicion and death. It seemed to him at times that there was in all Germans something decadent which worshiped death and looked upon suicide as an honorable and courageous thing. Had not the whole nation itself again and again since the time of Hermann the Red committed itself to suicide, binding its citizens together with ropes of deceit and vanity and injured pride to march to death against the legions of the world?

It was not only Germany he had escaped but this other corrupting thing, the love of destruction and death.

But he was puzzled still and his spirit, he knew, would never have peace until he understood what it was that happened on the night he hid himself in the very heart of the enemy in the lobby of the Grand Brunswick Hotel. He had to know. He had to believe that once what he saw was wrong. And so he said, "But you came to the hotel that night meaning to deliver me up to Fabrizius."

She looked away from him. "Yes," she said, "that is true. How could you know that?"

"I saw it as I sometimes see things. I knew that you were
not what they believed. You were not 'one of us.' Before
you came in I saw it all and I *knew*."

She began to cry and presently she said, "Yes, that was
true. For hours before I fought with myself. My brain and
my heart fought, like wild animals, inside me. On the one side
there was duty and family and country and the ideals they
had taught me, the only ones I ever knew. I had lived for
this triumph, the splendor of my country. I had risked my
life for it many times. It was for the New Germany, the new
order that I lived. On one side there was all that, on the
other there was only . . . you, ill, hunted, trapped beyond
escape. I thought, There is no way of saving him in any case.
The best I can do is take him to Fabrizius. There I have a little power. There perhaps I can help him. And so at last with
my heart beaten and choked I went to the hotel and passed
you and said, 'Excuse me. Now I must go to the railway
station.' That was my Judas kiss."

She was silent for a moment staring away from out of the
window at the brilliant sunlight over the lake. Behind the
lake the great mountains rose, white with snow against the
sky. He did not press her to go on. He waited, watching her,
understanding a little now why she was so changed, so still,
so dignified, so much more beautiful.

Presently in a low voice, still looking away from him, she
said, "It was a little thing that changed it all. It came the
moment I put my arm through yours and felt the warmth of
your body through the cloth of your uniform. Something
terrible happened. It was like the opening of the sea or the
falling away of the mountains. Quite suddenly we were the
only two people left in the world. In time and space, in the
darkness of that narrow street there was no one but you and
me. And a voice said, 'I will not do this thing. I will save him
—God alone knows why—but I will save him, and myself too
if it is possible!' Suddenly I hated passionately all those

things in which I had believed, all that world which had once seemed to me so glorious. I hated the men I had worshiped, the men I had cheered. I hated everything which before that moment had been my life, because you and I and the thing between us suddenly became more precious to me than the country or family or party or anything in the whole world. You and I, walking along the dark street in the snow, were more important than politicians or parties or wars or the German *Reich*. We were a man and a woman who loved each other standing alone at the beginning of the world, alone in time and space. No state, no party, no ideas had any rights which we were bound to respect, because we stood there together, a symbol of all humanity. No power had the right to destroy our happiness and our right to live. The same voice said, 'You may not be able to save him, but if he is caught you will be caught too. He will die but you will die with him,' and that was better than the other thing."

She was silent again for a moment. Then she said, "From that moment there was no longer any doubt. Now I am like a little naked child. I have left everything. I have nothing now but you, nothing on earth. I have betrayed everything I ever was before." Then she smiled, "But I do not mind. I am happy."

He pressed her hand against his cheek and said, "I am sorry now that I asked you. But I had to know . . . whether for once I had been wrong."

"No, you were not wrong. I came there meaning to betray you."

Then suddenly a flash of vision came to him. There would be a knock at the door and when she opened it there would be two Swiss policemen outside in long capes, one tall and heavy with a red mustache and the other a small dark man. And the tall one would say, "Excuse us, but we have come to inspect your papers." And they would look at the papers and say, "You will have to come with us to the inspector." Then the picture faded into a fog and after that he did not know what was to follow.

But it did not matter, even if they were interned and separated. They had escaped that awful nightmarish world. And what had happened to them had happened to all lovers since the beginning of time. Someday somewhere, when all the misery and suspicion and hate had abated a little, they could find a place where there was peace and decency and they could have the happiness God had meant for them since the beginning of time.

There was a knock at the door. She rose swiftly and went to open it. Beyond her in the hallway he saw two policemen in long capes, one tall and heavy with a red mustache, the other a small dark man. The tall one said, "Excuse us, but we have come to inspect your papers. . . ."

CUNNINGHAM

W. F. MORRIS

I first met Cunningham in the spring of 1916. It was outside the company headquarters' dugout one glorious day in June when the birds were singing as though there were no war within a hundred miles, and the familiar smell of chloride of lime and herded humanity was held temporarily in abeyance by the fresh early morning air. He had come up with the rations during the night to replace young Merton who had been knocked out during one of those raids our divisional headquarters were so fond of ordering.

I could see at a glance that he had been out before, and I liked the look of him as he stood there by the dugout steps, hands in pockets, pipe in mouth, and the old-pattern respirator satchel slung over one shoulder. The appearance of

a new member of the mess was always a matter of impor-
tance, for when half a dozen men are cooped up together
for what someone aptly described as long periods of intense
boredom punctuated by moments of intense fear, tempers
wore thin occasionally, and one man of the wrong sort
could create more mischief than the proverbial wagonload
of monkeys.

But it went deeper even than that. Most commanding
officers, I fancy, divided their juniors into two categories:
those who did merely what they were told, and those who
could be relied upon in an emergency to carry on upon
their own initiative. Unhealthy duties such as raids and
patrols were supposed to be allotted in rotation from a roster, but whenever it came to sending a party on some highly
dangerous and important job, ninety-nine commanding
officers out of a hundred would let the roster go hang and
put an officer from the second category in command. Now
as the number of names in this category was usually con-
siderably smaller than that in the other group, there was
undeniably a good deal of what is known as working the
willing horse, and it was therefore a matter of considerable
interest to all of us to see how a newcomer shaped.

Cunningham shaped well. He quickly graduated to that
select band of soldiers that is distinguished by no particular
rank—and by no kaleidoscope of chest colors for that matter—but possesses simply that little extra something that
the others have not got. The men, quick in such matters,
noticed it at once. Even the fussiest and jumpiest of them
were calm and happy if he were in charge of them, and the
usual good-natured blasphemy which the detailing of a
working or wiring party called forth became noticeably
milder when it was known that he was to lead it.

From the colonel downwards we were quickly satisfied
that Cunningham would "do" and we were the more glad to
have him because with the Somme battle approaching, we

knew that officers of his stamp were worth their weight in gold.

Cunningham and I hit it off very well together. We shared a brick-floored cottage room when we were back in rest, and on two memorable occasions, when the loan of a car enabled us to run into Amiens, we did ourselves superlatively well amid the varied wartime attractions of that remarkable city. Friendships in those days were usually strong but of short duration. One or the other would receive a Blighty wound, if nothing worse, and pass back down the lines never to be seen again. In our case, however, a slight mishap to one of us served only to strengthen the attachment.

For some days the battalion had been holding on to one of those graveyards of bare, blasted tree trunks and fallen branches that had been leafy woods less than a month before and, one morning just before dawn, it was discovered that Cunningham was missing. He had been out with a patrol which had returned safely, and he had last been seen no more than a few yards from the edge of the wood. It was certain he could not be far away, so I took a man with me and set out to look for him.

For twenty minutes we searched without success, but as soon as the light grew strong enough to see at all clearly, I spotted him out by a shell hole no more than a few yards from the margin of the wood. My runner, young Sanders, Cunningham's devoted servant, ran forward before I could stop him, but he went no more than a couple of paces. The light was still poor, but a man running upright makes a conspicuous target at under two hundred yards.

I crawled out to find young Sanders with a neat hole drilled in his forehead; death must have been instantaneous. I had begun to fear that Cunningham too was dead, but to my great relief as I wriggled up to him, he turned his head and and assured me that a broken arm was the full extent of the damage. It appeared that in the darkness he had tripped into a shell hole and broken his arm, and on trying to crawl out had become entangled in some low-pegged wire. With but one arm in commission, his struggles to free himself had resulted only in his becoming further entangled, and there he had remained fuming and helpless ever since.

I had with me a small but very efficient pair of wire cutters which had proved their worth on more than one occasion, and it took me no more than a few minutes to cut him free. Then we wriggled back to the shelter of the wood.

There was nothing heroic about this episode; it was no more dangerous than the ordinary daily round and common task of those hectic days above the Somme, but Cunningham chose to consider that I had saved his life. As a matter of fact I suppose I had, but it was those very efficient little wire cutters he had to thank, and the good luck that brought them with me.

With his arm in a sling he was of little use as a fighting soldier for the two or three weeks it took the bone to set, but he refused to go farther back than the transport lines and insisted on coming up to occupy a listening post we had established on the outskirts of Guillemont. He spoke German fluently, and on more than one occasion we had enjoyed a good laugh at some titbit of Teutonic humour he had overheard while lying inside the German wire.

Corps headquarters in due season heard of this accomplishment and inevitably they took him from us. The colonel fought a gallant rearguard action to defend our rights and, nobly backed up by the brigadier, put down a heavy barrage of indignant chits on headquarters. But it was all in vain. Cunningham received orders to report to corps intelligence for duty at the prisoners' cage in the interrogation of prisoners.

After two years of trench warfare most men would have

jumped at the chance of the comparative safety and lux-
urious comfort of headquarters life; but not so Cunningham. But orders were orders; he had to go. We gave him a
great send-off and besought him half seriously not to forget
us when he was a brass-hatted general with rows of deco-
rations, for like most infantrymen we were firmly convinced
that the farther one went from the line, the greater became
one's chances of promotion and honors.

And so he departed for the august portals of corps HQ,
and as though to emphasize the gulf that had now come
between us, a large green staff car came to fetch him away.
We did see him again, however, for twice he visited us when
we were back in rest, and occasionally one of us drawing
money from the field cashier ran into him in the little
market town behind our front. Then the division was
shifted northwards to another corps and we lost sight of
him for good.

The history of our battalion from that time onward did
not differ materially from that of any other. We went into
the line for our tours of duty and we came back for our
rests; we tramped out of Arras one day over seven hundred
strong and returned three days later with a little under two
hundred; we had one glorious fortnight in a sleepy village
in the back area where we lay on our backs by a stream in
the sunshine and had new-laid eggs and cream for breakfast; then new faces crowded in on us and we marched out
again at full strength towards the old familiar rumble.
Christmas 1917 came and went and with it rumors of a
great German spring offensive.

It is unnecessary to repeat the story of that great attack;
it is now a matter of history that all may read. My own part
in it was short and ignominious. I remember days of anxious
waiting—surely the most trying of all a soldier's jobs—and I
remember being awakened in the small hours by a tremen-
dous cannonade and muttering to myself, "Thank God it's

come at last!" as I felt for my flashlight and scrambled off the wire-netting bunk.

Outside it was cold and dark and misty and very noisy. Most of our deeply buried telephone lines had gone already, and it was difficult to get any trustworthy information. We stood to in our scattered posts and waited for the deluge.

Dawn came at last, gray and cold and misty, and presently we knew by the lengthening range of the German barrage and the distant clatter of machine guns that their storm troops had gone over. But none of us knew what was really happening, though conflicting reports and rumors were plentiful.

After a cup of hot tea I set off to visit some outlying posts and gather if possible some definite information. Some of the posts, I found, had already beaten off one or more attacks; others had not even seen a German. On the face of it, this seemed highly satisfactory, but the clatter of machine guns, unmistakably German, sounding from two directions well behind our front, gave pause to any hasty optimism. As the newspapers have it, the situation was obscure.

The mist lifted somewhat as the morning advanced, and from a Lewis-gun post above a sunken road I had my first sight that day of the enemy. They were no more than three hundred yards off and streaming towards us, not in closely packed ranks as in earlier offensives, but in little blobs and files.

That particular attack lasted no more than a bare half hour, and I know from personal observation it suffered heavily. The dozen odd men in the little post were jubilant, but I was not so happy myself. I caught glimpses now and again of those little blobs and files among the folds of the country to right and left. It was clear that several of our posts had been scuppered and that the enemy were steadily penetrating our front by way of the dead ground between those posts which still held out.

I held on for another hour and then decided to send the gun back about half a mile to a place I knew of that commanded a shallow valley where there seemed to be considerable enemy movement.

The post we held must be described, however. A sunken road crossed the side of a hill from the slope of which there was a very good field of fire. Some ten yards from the road a redoubt had been dug on the hillside and wired all round. In this redoubt was a perpendicular shaft some twelve feet deep leading to a low tunnel which came out on the sunken road behind.

The men went off under the sergeant while I remained to have a last look round. I stayed no more than three minutes at the most; then I slipped my glasses into the case, went down the rough ladder, and groped my way along the tunnel. As I came out into the sunken road, stooping to avoid the low lintel, I cannoned into a man standing by the entrance. My eyes were dazzled after the darkness of the tunnel, and thinking the man was Sergeant Rowland, I started cursing him for having left the men; but I stopped suddenly with dropped jaw when I saw that he was wearing a scuttle-shaped helmet and field gray. An automatic pistol was pressing gently against my ribs, a hand pulled my revolver from the holster, and my share in the great offensive was at an end.

In due course and with many halts and questionings by the way I came at length to a prison camp in northern Bavaria. There life assumed once more an ordered monotony. We took exercise, read what books were to be had, groused about the food, had fierce arguments about trifling matters, found hilarious enjoyment in playing practical jokes on a pompous little German lieutenant of the reserve, took up hobbies with the enthusiasm of schoolboys and dropped them as quickly, separated into cliques, and were intensely bored; in fact it was the same old war, intense monotony but without the periods of excitement and danger.

I became friends with a gunner captain named Benson. He confided to me one day that he had made up his mind to escape. He needed a partner for the venture and thought that I might be the man. I was; and from that moment I ceased to be bored.

Benson had been collecting the necessary kit for some time and by various subterfuges had amassed a treasure consisting of a complete civilian outfit, maps, compass, concentrated food, German money, and a pair of homemade wire cutters. He had been learning German and had made considerable progress, and he was delighted when he found that I too had a smattering of the language. Actually my knowledge was confined to a very limited number of useful phrases I had picked up from Cunningham, but on the other hand I have a good ear for copying sounds, and I had been told on more than one occasion that my accent was very nearly perfect. We proposed to travel by night and avoid all contact with the people of the country, but we hoped our German would be good enough to carry us through a chance encounter.

My first task was to make or acquire a civilian outfit. I succeeded in dyeing a pair of khaki slacks a nondescript color in a fearsome mixture of ink and boot polish and set about converting a service tunic into a civilian jacket by removing the pockets and buttons.

Benson had already formed the rough outlines of a plan of escape, and the all-important details were gradually beginning to fall into place. It will suffice to say that the plan was based upon a very careful study of the routine of the camp and a diversion to be staged by some boisterous spirits at the critical moment. We were confident that helpers for this part of the plan would not be wanting when the time came.

Then just when everything was shaping well, disaster descended upon us. Benson was playing deck tennis one afternoon on an asphalt court when in jumping for a high ring he slipped and fell. A broken leg takes six weeks or more to mend, and for some time after that he would be in no condition to tackle a long and exhausting march across country.

It could not be helped. We should have to possess our souls in patience and wait till he was fit again. But he would have none of it. He urged me to take his kit and find another partner or carry on by myself. He pointed out that he would probably be sent to the military hospital more than thirty miles away and might never return to that particular camp. In any case it would be impossible for him to smuggle his escaping kit with him, and therefore it was only common sense for me to take it and carry on.

He left the camp that night for the hospital. It seemed to me as if the bottom had been knocked out of my world. My one absorbing interest was gone, and in spite of his arguments I had not the heart to carry on without him. For two days I mooned about the camp by myself completely at a loose end. I did not try to find another partner; I gave up all idea of attempting to escape. Then chance took a hand.

Half a dozen officers arrived one day to inspect the camp. Such inspections were not infrequent, and we derived considerable amusement from them by watching, and occasionally innocently retarding, the feverish efforts of the camp staff to impress the visitors. On this occasion, however, no untoward incident occurred, but in the course of my prowling round the camp later that afternoon I chanced to pass close by the kommandantur and saw through the open door the caps and greatcoats of the inspecting officers hanging in a row on the pegs in the passage. Evidently the visitors had stayed on for a drink and possibly a meal.

I passed on slowly but with my heart beating like a hammer, for it had come to me suddenly that in one of those coats and caps I would have a sporting chance of marching unchallenged out of the camp.

After Benson's departure I had given up all idea of escape, and I acted now on the spur of the moment. I turned and came back slowly, whistling and with my hands in my pockets. I gave one quick glance round and shot up the steps. My luck was in; the passage was empty. It would have been madness to have attempted to carry the clothes across the open square in broad daylight, but there was a window in the passage giving on to a small waste piece of ground backed by a high wall. I opened the window quietly, took the coat and cap from the nearest peg, and threw them out. Then I closed the window and slipped back down the steps.

The whole operation had taken less than half a minute. I was jubilant; but I had yet to retrieve the coat and cap from the waste ground and convey them to some place where I could put them on after I had changed into civilian clothes. What had been done had been done on the spur of the moment, and I had no plan, but as I strolled along thinking matters over, chance came again to my aid.

Two British orderlies from the adjacent Tommies' camp were crossing the square carrying a large laundry basket between them. I knew one of the men to be a good fellow who would probably be willing to help, and I turned slightly to the right so that our courses converged. "If you want to do me a good turn," I said quietly as we came near, "follow me and say nothing." The good fellow gave me one intelligent look and followed without a word. I strolled round the angle of the main building and up the side, where I was out of sight of the square, to the door of the waste piece of ground. The two orderlies with the basket followed me through.

Under the frosted glass window lay the coat and cap. I picked them up and began to whisper a word of explanation to the two orderlies; but at the sight of the German uniform, Red, the fellow I knew, just grinned and lifted the cover of the basket without a word. I pushed the coat and cap inside.

"March across past the back of the latrine by the side gate," I whispered, "but give me a minute to get there first." The two men grinned again and nodded, and with a word of thanks I strolled off towards the latrine.

As luck would have it, no one was there, though it hardly mattered, since none of my fellow prisoners would have given me away. I waited till I heard the orderlies' footsteps at the back and then I went out. The little building screened the spot from the rest of the square, though one of the sentries on the wire fence was in sight. Fortunately he had his back turned, and in a moment I had whipped the cap and coat from the laundry basket and shot back into the latrine. The orderlies, admirable fellows, continued imperturbably on their way.

I hid my spoil behind a cistern and strolled back as casually as I could to the main building. Up in my room I retrieved poor old Benson's escaping kit from its various hiding places, put on the civilian clothes, and pulled on my uniform over the top, while Grey, the only one of my roommates who happened to be present, looked on with interest.

"Heading for home?" he asked laconically at last. I nodded as I stuffed the maps in an inside pocket. "Want any help?" I told him I would be grateful if he could manage to cover my absence from the evening roll call so as to give me as big a start as possible. He promised to see to it.

I had decided that the best time to make the attempt was at dusk when the daylight was failing and the big arcs surrounding the camp were still unlighted. The German is a most orderly animal, as I have proved to my own satisfaction more than once during the course of the war. The camp lights were switched on every night three quarters of an hour after sunset to the minute, and I knew that if I timed my attempt ten minutes earlier, I should run no danger of being caught by the lights.

Unfortunately there was still half an hour to go, and I was in a fever of impatience. That half hour was the longest I ever spent. Every moment I expected to hear the uproar that would announce that the visiting officers had finished their tippling and had discovered the loss of the coat and cap. But the longest wait must have an end and at last it was time to go.

Grey went with me. Trying to look as unconcerned as possible, we strolled slowly across to the latrines. As luck would have it they were empty. I tore off my uniform and put on the German greatcoat and cap. I had the maps, food, compass, and money bestowed in various pockets of my civilian clothes; a trilby hat was rolled up in my trouser pocket. Grey gave me a final look-over to see that all was well, pulled the cap to a more rakish angle, and as a final touch stuck his watch crystal in my eye as a monocle. Then he went out to see if the coast was clear, for we were close to the side gate and it would never do for the sentry there to see a German officer issuing from the prisoners' latrines.

I stood in the shadow of the entrance and waited, trying hard to keep calm; waiting is always so much more difficult than action. Perhaps a minute went by, or maybe two, and then at last I heard him call that the sentry's back was turned. It was now or never.

I stepped out from my shelter, gave him a wink as I passed, and headed for the gate.

My heart was beating like a hammer, but I strutted along with a lord-of-all creation air and tried to look as Prussian as I could. The sentry did not see me till I was close to the gate, and then for a moment he did nothing. I thought that he had recognized me and that the game was up; but suddenly he came to life and began to fumble with the lock. I stared at him coldly through my monocle, which combined with my stony silence and haughty air seemed to fluster him so that he took a long time to open the gate. Meanwhile I was in a cold fear that the man would recognize me.

At last he had the gate open. I passed through; but there still remained the gate in the outer wire to be opened, and he fumbled badly with that too. It was really a comic situation, for the poor man was even more scared than I was. But the second gate also was open at last, and I passed through it with a lordly acknowledgement of the sentry's salute.

The camp was surrounded by woods, and my first impulse was to dive for the shelter of the undergrowth; but I realized that my only chance of avoiding recapture was to get beyond them before my escape was discovered, for once a cordon were thrown around the woods, escape from them would be difficult. Therefore I walked down the road at a moderate pace till I was out of sight of the camp; then I dived in among the undergrowth, tore off the German coat and cap with feverish haste, put on the trilby, and emerged as an inconspicuous civilian. The road would take me beyond the woods more quickly than a winding woodland path, and as time was the all-important factor, I set off along the road again at my best speed.

I did not breathe really freely till I came to the end of the trees and saw the open sky above me. I took a deep breath then, pulled out my map and compass, and set a course by the stars. I kept going steadily all night, skirting the villages, and by dawn when I lay in a copse to sleep, I had put many miles between myself and the camp.

There is no need to give the details of that nightmare

march, for a nightmare it became after the first few days. I marched at night and slept in hiding during the day. Twice at dusk I bought food in village shops, and I tried to mask any imperfections of language and accent by tying a handkerchief round my face and feigning a toothache.

I was heading for the Dutch frontier on the course Benson and I had worked out together, but by the ninth day I had begun to wonder if I would ever make it. The cold nights, exposure to bad weather, and the poor food had tried my strength severely, and the wire fence guarding the Dutch frontier which we had so cheerfully decided could present no real obstacle to determined men, seemed to grow more formidable with every mile I traveled.

One morning just before dawn as I dropped exhausted in the shelter of a wood, I knew that I could never reach the frontier now on foot. But I told myself that I was not done yet. The Rhine was only a few miles off, and if I could reach the river and find a Dutch bargeman, it might be possible to bribe the man to smuggle me across the frontier in his barge. I was happier after that decision and I slept like a log all day.

I reached the river the following night after a comparatively easy march and began my search for a Dutch barge. But I failed to find one. A few German barges were moored along the bank—the port of registration painted on each told their nationality—but no Dutch.

While I lay in hiding the next day I did some hard thinking. A short distance lower down the river lay Cologne with large docks and many barges, and among them surely at least one Dutch. It was unfortunate that the city and docks were on the opposite bank of the river and to reach them I should have to cross a bridge, but that was a risk I was prepared to face. If the bridge were guarded it would be foolish to attempt to cross it at night when few wayfarers were about, but during the day I hoped it might be possible to slip across unchallenged among the crowd.

On the following morning I walked boldly into that suburb of Cologne that stands on the east bank of the river. I walked with a stiff leg and very square shoulders, as I thought that the role of a discharged wounded soldier was the best to adopt; and with my worn face and clothes hanging loosely about my emaciated body I must have looked the part to perfection.

A little short of the bridge I came upon a group of people waiting on the pavement. A tramcar rattled up as I pushed my way among them and I was carried forward with the rush. Acting on the impulse of the moment, I climbed inside and took my seat with the rest. Several of the passengers read newspapers and paid their fares in silence, and when the conductress came to me, I held out a few *pfennigs* as the others had done and received my ticket without having to utter a word. The tram rumbled on over the great bridge, and a few minutes later I got down unmolested in the shadow of the great cathedral.

After my long solitude it was a strange and exciting experience to find myself walking the streets of a busy city, but no one of that hurrying throng took any notice of me, and as time passed my confidence grew. I searched along the river bank and the docks for a Dutch barge and found three, but each had many men about her loading or unloading, and it would have been suicidal to have approached a skipper there in broad daylight and put him to the test. I therefore decided to return after dark and try to creep aboard unseen.

I went back into the town and wandered about the busy streets. The fine shops fascinated me; it was many months since I had seen anything bigger than a village store, and I lingered in front of the plate-glass windows like an urchin asking for a packet of cigarettes, when without apparent reason I became acutely aware of two men standing near me. One tall and the other short, both dressed in civilian clothes, they had stopped for a moment to look at the shop window. Something vaguely familiar in the bearing of one of them fixed my attention. The shorter of the two had already turned away, and as the other followed him, he looked in my direction and our eyes met.

Recognition is as swift as the fastest camera shutter and may be equally revealing. It was Cunningham. I was taken completely by surprise, but I flatter myself that I gave no more than a slight start. As for Cunningham, not an eyelid flickered, not a muscle of his face moved, nor did he arrest the turning of his head for the fraction of a second; only the momentary spark in his eye betrayed his recognition. He went off beside his companion, chatting in German as though he had seen nothing. That sight of Cunningham heartened me. It was comforting to know that there was even one fellow countryman of mine in this great city. If he could play so gallantly his dangerous game, of which the penalty of failure was death, it would be shameful for me to falter in a game for lower stakes. I congratulated myself that I had made no sudden exclamation, and I was glad that his companion's back had been turned at the moment of recognition, for even my slight start might have given us away. I realized then the self-control and courage needed by the successful spy. My own wanderings as a fugitive had given me some inkling of the utter loneliness of the work and of the self-reliance needed for the part.

I wandered down to the riverside again, and as I stood in the dusk gazing out across the water, a man came and leant on the rail beside me. It was the one thing I had been afraid of—that some loiterer would try to get into conversation with me; but as I turned hastily to move away I caught a glimpse of his profile. It was Cunningham's.

"Oh, it's you," I said with relief.

He nodded.

"Is this safe?" I asked. "I don't want to get you in a mess."

He looked at me curiously. "How do you mean?" he asked.

"Well, I'm only an escaped prisoner," I said, "and if I'm caught it's the prisoner-of-war camp again; but for you. . . ." I laughed shortly. "I suppose it would be the traditional firing squad at dawn."

He gave me an odd look that made me feel like an ingenue at a party who has said the wrong thing. I suppose intelligence men have their own etiquette of what is good luck and what is bad luck, like airmen, and after all it was only natural that a reference to a firing squad at dawn should be one of the things that was not "done." Anyway, I felt a fool.

"So you have escaped from a prison camp, have you! Stout fellow!" he said in the old friendly manner. "Tell me about it." I told him. "You've had a rough time," he commented at the end. "It must have taken a bit of guts."

"Guts!" I echoed. "*You* talk of guts! Why, half an hour of your job would reduce me to a nervous wreck."

He let that pass without comment, nor did he volunteer any information about his job or his life since he left his comfortable intelligence post behind the lines for the hazardous one there in Germany. And I did not question him. I had heard enough about intelligence to know that agents worked so secretly that often they did not know one another even.

He asked me about my future plans. I told him of my original intention and of my change of plan. He thought I was wise to have abandoned the idea of footing it to Holland. The frontier was closely watched and guarded by live wire in places; without special knowledge of the district I would have hardly stood a chance. But he shook his head

over the other plan also. Of course there were Dutch barge-
men who would be willing to smuggle an escaped prisoner
across the frontier, but there must be many more who would
not take the risk. My difficulty would be to find the right
man; if I approached the wrong one first I should be in the
cart.

I asked what he advised. He was silent for a few moments. "I think I can help you," he said at last. "You had
better come to my rooms for the night while I arrange it.
You will be all right there."

I said I had no intention of adding to the obvious risks he
ran, but he laughed and assured me it would be all right. "I
owe you something, anyway," he said. "If you wander about
Cologne all night, someone will talk to you, and then the
game will be up. And besides you are in no fit condition to
do that; what you need is a square meal and a bed. But I
must see that the coast is clear first. Meanwhile, I advise
you to keep on the move; I'll be back in half an hour." And
with that he turned and left me.

I kept on the move as he had advised, and returned to the
spot on the riverbank as soon as the half hour was up. But
there was no sign of Cunningham. He was, I knew, a man of
his word, and as the minutes went by without his putting in
an appearance, my anxiety can be imagined.

Exhaustion can play strange tricks with the most equable
temperament. After my meeting with Cunningham and his
offer of help I had soared from a state not far removed from
despair to one of rosy optimism; now I was sliding rapidly
back again. Something had gone amiss; not only did I see
that promised square meal recede into the distance and the
prison camp loom near, but I heard in imagination the very
volley that would end Cunningham's career. All this because he had delayed ten minutes beyond the appointed
time. It will be seen that I was pretty near the end of my
tether.

He came at last, and gave some explanation of his delay which I failed to hear in my joy at seeing him. He told me the coast was clear; he would go ahead and I was to follow a few paces behind. In this way we went back into the town, up one of the main streets, down a side turning, and in through an open door. He led me up a short flight of stairs and through a small hall to a comfortably furnished room. After locking the door he put food and wine before me and sat smoking his pipe while I ate. And how I ate.

Afterwards we talked of old times, of the old battalion and of days in France. Then I had a glorious hot bath and he put me into a little bedroom opening off the hall. It was a spare room, he said, and was never used. He would be out all night, but he would lock the door and I would be quite safe. A woman would come in to tidy up in the morning, but she would not trouble me. My room had always been kept locked, and if I kept quiet she would not know I was there. He could not say exactly when he could give me breakfast—as though that mattered—but he gave me a loaf and some meat in case I was hungry. Then with a cheery good night he closed and locked the door. I heard him go out some minutes later.

Contrary to expectations I did not sleep well; the bed was too soft and comfortable after my spell of hard living, but I dropped off before dawn and awoke to hear the woman bustling about the flat. After she had gone, I dressed and ate some of the meat and bread.

I found it dull sitting there in that little room, and I wished that Cunningham had thought of locking the door on the inside instead of on the outside, so that I could have gone into the other room and amused myself with the German illustrated papers I had seen there the night before. Except for a floor rug, a chair, a cupboard, and a bed, the room was bare. It amused me, however, to think that an English intelligence man should have his own flat in Cologne and even a spare room in which to entertain his fellow countrymen. In the cupboard I found a bag with an old label for Berlin and the name H. von Goburg written on it in Cunningham's handwriting. That too was amusing, but a grim jest for him if it were seen through.

It was nearly midday when he returned. He apologized for keeping me shut up so long, but said he had not been idle. And indeed he had not.

It was, as he had said, almost impossible to get across the Dutch frontier if one did not know the ropes, but on the other hand it was a fairly simple matter for those who did. Actually the frontier was crossed pretty frequently by smugglers and others, and to cut a long story short, he had arranged for one who was an expert at the game to take me over that night. I was to catch the evening train to Aachen where he would hand me over to the frontier expert. Before dawn I would be on Dutch soil.

He brushed aside my objections to his coming with me; the risk to himself, he said, was negligible, and with my limited knowledge of German I could not possibly risk the journey alone. And besides it was all arranged.

So I thanked him gratefully and sat down to the excellent cold meal he had prepared.

He had to be busy all that afternoon again, but before he went he handed me a suit from his wardrobe and put me back into my little room. "We can't have you looking too much like a tramp." He laughed. I suggested he might let me have the run of the flat, but he said that was too risky as the woman had a key. So back I went to the little room and was locked in.

It was good to feel well dressed again. Cunningham and I were much the same size and the suit was a tolerably good fit. His *nom de guerre*, H. von Goburg, was written on the tab of the jacket below the name of a Berlin tailor. Now at least the cut of my clothes could not give me away.

Somehow I whiled away that interminable time of waiting. I had brought with me the German illustrated papers
and they helped. The captions were not easy to follow, but
the rather low humor of the pictures was obvious enough.

It was nearly eight o'clock when he returned. I laughed
aloud when he opened the door, for he was dressed in the
uniform of a German officer and looked a typical Prussian.
He said it would save us from being bothered by petty officials. I laughed again and reminded him that I had adopted
the same plan at the prison camp and with satisfactory re-
sults.

He had a taxi waiting outside, so that we drove to the
station in style, and all the way I was grinning to myself at
the thought of what the people on the crowded pavements
would have said if they had known who we really were. He
carried the whole thing off magnificently; he paid the taxi
man with a lordly air and marched up the platform to a first-
class carriage with just the right swagger. Two other people
were in the compartment, but they did not worry us. I sat
undisturbed in my corner and pretended to read the maga-
zine he had brought me.

The journey to Aachen was short and passed off without
incident. Cunningham's uniform brought him salutes and
respect, and carried us through the barrier without question. We walked from the station through the lighted
streets of the town and out along a country road. Away to
the left a lighted tramcar moved slowly on its way; ahead
the red and green signal lights of a railway glowed through
the darkness.

I remember feeling strangely unreal; it seemed absurd
that this commonplace road could lead to freedom.

A man lounging by a gateway gave us a good night as we
passed. Cunningham halted suddenly and gripped my hand.
"Follow him," he whispered with a nod towards the dark
figure. "He will see you through. Good-by." Before I had

recovered from my surprise he was several yards away striding back down the road.

That was the last I ever saw of Cunningham. I dared not call out or run after him. I could only turn sadly towards the dark figure by the gate. All my elation at the nearness of success had left me; it seemed a shameful thing that I should go on towards safety and freedom while he who had arranged it all was striding through the darkness back to his lonely, dangerous work.

The man by the gate turned without a word as I approached. He led me by a large dark house and through a hedge at the end of a long garden. After that we went very cautiously; sometimes we crawled, and once we lay still while two men passed close to us. Then we halted beyond a ditch on the edge of a small field. I could distinguish a narrow footpath winding toward a low building with one dimly lighted window.

I was just wondering when we should reach the wire and how we would cross it, when my guide put his lips to my ear and spoke for the first time. "You are now in Holland," he said. "Go straight ahead to the house." And before I could ask a question or even thank him he had turned and disappeared back the way we had come.

I shall not try to describe my feeling at that moment or the many little kindnesses of the friendly Dutch guards at the little house when they had satisfied themselves that I was really an escaped prisoner of war. I had a great reception from many British residents in Holland and from the British authorities to whom I reported. Everyone treated me as though I were a hero, and I felt very mean in taking all the credit to myself, for I thought it would be most unwise to mention Cunningham to anyone except an accredited intelligence officer. Madison, the one man I gathered I could have spoken freely to, was on leave in London and I did not see any of the higher embassy officials.

One of the juniors came to the station to see me off for
England, and as we stood chatting by the carriage door he
said, "Madison will want to see you when you get to town.
He will be interested to hear you have been in Cologne."
Then with a quick glance round and lowered voice he went
on, "His department has had a spot of bother in that region
lately. Two of our people have gone silent—and have disappeared."

A sudden chill came over me as I realized the meaning of
his words; I thought of Cunningham back there in the centre of the danger. "You mean . . . ?" I began.

He nodded. "I'm afraid so. You see, the Huns have got a
new man on counterespionage in that area. A pretty live
wire from all accounts. They say he's played the game
himself behind our lines and knows every move. . . ." Then
he added brightly as the train began to move, "A dangerous
bloke—von Goburg is his name, Captain von Goburg, blast
him! Well, good-by, and good luck."

THE ENVELOPE

J. STORER CLOUSTON

"My word!" exclaimed the general. "This is deuced different from traveling on the Highland line before the war!"

"Very, sir," the young guardsman agreed.

"You know this country then?"

"I sometimes used to shoot at a place in Sutherland-shire, sir."

"Well," said the general, a stout affable warrior with a row of ribbons on his broad chest, "except when I was in India, I've shot and fished in Scotland every year since I was a boy. How many times I've been up and down this Highland line I'd be afraid to say; and, by Jove, what a contrast now!"

"Just what I was thinking, sir," said the young officer.

"Not a lady to be seen!" continued the general. "Not a keeper, not a dog; not a gun or a rod or any other mortal thing one used to see here. Everybody's in uniform; and even then you've got to get a pass like a ticket-of-leave man! The piping days of peace seem far enough away, what?"

One of the two young Australians at the other end of the carriage took his cigar out of his mouth and joined in the conversation. There was none of the guardsman's well-drilled air of deference about this young man. His manner was engagingly frank and direct.

"This is my first trip to the Highlands of Scotland," said he, "and a mighty nice country to go fishing and shooting in it looks. I suppose the whole place used just to be crawling with tourists and sportsmen and guys collecting butterflies and birds' eggs. Not much prohibited area about it then, I guess!"

"The rummiest thing about the whole show," put in the R.N.R. lieutenant, "is not being able to get a drink whenever you want. Just fancy being in the home of whisky and having to wet your whistle with tea!"

There were these five officers in the carriage: the burly conversational general; the two young Australians—one, who had just spoken, tall and thin with very black hair and a long nose; the other, a quieter young man, of the fair, blue-eyed, stolid type; the R.N.R. lieutenant, a plain-looking freckled man with a wide mouth; and the young guardsman, with a captain's stars and the grenadier's cap band, spruce and slender, a type of the *pukka* army officer. And there was also one civilian, a quiet looking man with a beard, who had begun by joining in the general conversation, mentioning incidentally that he was an official of the board of agriculture traveling on business, and then had put on a pair of spectacles and become deeply immersed in a mass of papers, apparently official correspondence. A small blotting pad lay on his knee, and every now and then he seemed to be scribbling notes with a fountain pen.

The six had found themselves together in this first-class compartment after passengers from the South had changed trains at Inverness and passed the barrier at the southern limit of the military area.

"What's the use in this prohibited area anyhow?" demanded the tall Australian. "Seems to me it gives a peaceful fighting man a lot of trouble for no particular object I can see."

The general laughed in his bluff way.

"They evidently don't think all fighting men are peaceful," said he.

"Yes, but see here, sir," argued the R.N.R. lieutenant, "it seems to me all very well for civilians to have passports, but isn't the King's uniform a good enough passport?"

The general coughed discreetly, pursed his lips, and then, like one revealing a little more than he had any business to, said, "I may tell you I had a talk with a somewhat important police official in Edinburgh, and he says that the King's uniform has more than once been the passport for quite the wrong sort of gentlemen."

"Black sheep in wolf's clothing," suggested the tall Australian.

The others laughed, all except the civilian, who still seemed absorbed in his papers, and the guardsman, who murmured, "What a beastly idea! I didn't know that game was being played in this country."

"I assure you it is," said the general emphatically. "At least, I have the very best authority possible. That's why they're so particular about these passports. They looked at mine so long, I began to think they were going to arrest me!" He turned to the civilian and inquired, "I suppose even government officials have got to go through the same thing?"

The man with the beard looked up and nodded.

"They don't let any of us off," said he. "In fact, a civilian's passport, even if he be an official, is a much more complicated affair than a soldier's."

"In other words," said the general shrewdly, "a soldier's passport is probably easier to fake."

Again the board of agriculture official nodded.

"In all probability that's an added advantage of traveling in uniform," said he.

"Meaning if one is the kind of black sheep we were speaking of!" said the sailor. "Well, I suppose there's something in that."

"There's such an infernal lot of exaggeration in everything one hears nowadays," the general declared, "that I take what my friend in the police told me with a grain of salt. Forging a passport and all the rest of it isn't such an easy game; I wouldn't like to play it myself!"

"And what is there to be learned when one does get into this military area place?" asked the fair Australian. "It doesn't look to me as though there was much to be seen so far."

"Two naval bases, Cromarty and Scapa," said the guardsman.

"And the northwest corner of Scotland is said to have possibilities for the undesirable visitory," added the government official, looking up quickly from his papers.

The fair Australian stretched himself, and laughed. "I thought there were only mountains and stags out that way!"

"So there are, inland," said the general. "Grand deerstalking country too!"

He turned to the guardsman and launched forth into sporting reminiscences, while the young officers listened, and the civilian went on jotting down notes, till at last, at one of the incessant stations, the breezy general jumped up and cried, "Hullo! I ought to get out here!"

It was an old-fashioned carriage, with no corridor, and, besides the six passengers, its contents seemed to be chiefly the general's belongings. Two of his bags were on the seats, and more loaded the rack. The grenadier captain lent a hand in clearing this collection on to the platform, and, to make room, the civilian stepped out, strolled a few paces along the train, and stood by waiting. A couple of minutes later they were off again.

"We've got a little more room now," said the civilian, pulling a small suitcase from under the seat and placing it beside him.

"Our friend, the brass hat, pretty well filled the whole place." The tall Australian laughed. "I guess I'll make myself a little more comfortable too," he said.

There was a general movement in the carriage, each of the five either shifting his seat or moving his belongings. The grenadier and the two Australians put on their overcoats, and the government official took a rug from a bundle and threw it over his knees. As they all settled down at last, the tall Australian remarked, "Well, now one can stretch one's legs, at—"

He meant, it seemed, to have added "last," but his speech was arrested in the midst. He caught the grenadier's eye and then the civilian's. Each had seen the same thing. It was the Australian who picked it up from the floor—a torn and crumpled envelope, but the writing on it singularly legible.

"Here's a queer address to find in the prohibited area!" said he with a short laugh.

The civilian and the grenadier were now sitting in corners opposite to one another, and he held out the envelope so that both could read it. Over his shoulder the fair Australian and the R.N.R. lieutenant were reading it too. Of the name, only the last syllable "stein" remained, and below it was the address, "Königstrasse 13, Köln."

For a moment nobody spoke, and then the sailor asked, "Anybody here claim this pretty thing?"

But nobody answered him.

"Wow!" exclaimed the tall Australian suddenly. "It must have been dropped by old brass hat!"

The grenadier answered quickly and warmly, "Never! That was General Fawkes-Turing! He didn't know me, of course, but I knew him well enough. He's absolutely above suspicion!"

"Suspicion!" said the fair Australian. "You really call this suspicious then?"

"Don't you?"

Again nobody spoke for a moment, and then in a quiet, rather hesitating voice, the civilian said, "I suppose, perhaps, the fact that nobody acknowledges it, does—er—seem a little odd."

"There's nothing inside the envelope," said the fair Australian. "It's just a dirty scrap of paper."

"That's what started us into this war, my son!" said his friend. "Scraps of paper have taken a new lease of life since August 1914. Still, there'd be nothing so very much in this scrap to incriminate a fellow—if it wasn't, as this gentleman remarked, that nobody is willing to acknowledge it."

"Couldn't it have been in the carriage all the time?" suggested the R.N.R. lieutenant. "Under the seat, for instance?"

The tall Australian looked round the carriage at each in turn, and then at the envelope.

"I suppose it's quite possible," said he slowly.

"But you mean we can hardly take it for granted?" asked the civilian in the same diffident voice.

The other gave a short laugh. "Well, if you put it like that. . . ."

"Oh, I only supposed you meant that!" said the civilian hurriedly.

There was another pause, and then the grenadier said, "We were all moving about the carriage. It's quite clear we can't tell who dropped this thing."

"Assuming any of us did," added the fair Australian.

"My son," said his tall friend, "that's the only assumption we can go on, just at present anyhow, till we get things cleared up a bit."

He looked round the company, and then as the others seemed to be waiting instinctively for his opinion, he went on, "There are just three possible solutions, seems to me. Either the old brass hat did drop this, whatever his name is—"

"Impossible!" reiterated the guardsman warmly.

"Excuse me, my friend," said the other soothingly, "there's no point in getting gingery. The old boy may have had something wrapped up in it. It says nothing against him, seeing that he hasn't denied owning it. We've got to reckon on the chance of this being a mare's nest, just as we've got to reckon on the chance of the other thing."

"Hear, hear!" said the sailor, beginning to fill a pipe.

"I see," agreed the guardsman. "Yes, of course that's possible. Still. . . ."

"I'm coming to that *still*." The Australian smiled. "Well, now, that's the first solution. The second is, that it was in the carriage before any of us got in at Inverness. And the third is, that one of us dropped it and won't own up. Well now, with those three solutions all open, what can we do?"

"I quite see," said the civilian. "Yes, that puts the matter very well. And so you say you propose to go on the only assumption possible?"

"I'm just putting the case to the company. It's not for me to propose."

"Oh, I was only thinking of what you said before," said the board of agriculture official hurriedly. "But of course, if you think we ought to go on any other assumption—well —er—certainly suggest one."

"I certainly don't suggest anything different from what I said before," replied the Australian emphatically.

"And what did you suggest before?" asked the sailor.

"This gentleman seems to be taking down my remarks in shorthand," said the Australian, nodding towards the agricultural official, with a pleasantly ironical smile, and yet with something significant in his eye as it rested on the civilian's papers and writing pad.

"Oh, no, I assure you this is merely a little official correspondence," said the civilian with what seemed meant for a laugh. "I speak merely from recollection of this officer's remarks. They seemed to be very reasonable."

The grenadier cut in abruptly, "I say that we must obviously all regard ourselves as under suspicion."

"Precisely," said the tall Australian. "That's exactly my point. I say that's the only safe assumption in the meanwhile. The question is—what are we to do?"

"Supposing I arrest you, and this gentleman arrests me, and so on till we all arrest each other?" suggested the R.N.R. lieutenant.

There was only half a laugh from the Australians and the civilian, and the grenadier never even smiled. Evidently the situation struck them all as having passed the jesting stage. Their eyes wandered furtively from one to another of their companions, and—so far as their expressions revealed their minds—the same thought seemed to be equally behind each glance—"There is probably a spy in this carriage."

Once again the tall Australian broke the silence.

"Someone's got to speak out," said he, "and I'll begin. What do we know of each other? That's the first question. Well, my name's Mackay and my friend here is called Sutherland; or at least he says he is. We only met at King's

Cross Station, but he says he knows some of my folk out in Sydney and I happen to know some of his—that's to say, if they are the Sutherlands he says they are. *If* his tale is a true bill, I can answer for his people being as good citizens and fine folk as any in Australia. While if his tale isn't true, well, all I can say is he's a kind of magician, for what he doesn't seem to know about Sydney and the Sydney Sutherlands isn't worth knowing."

He looked towards his fellow Australian, who nodded and said, "That's all right. That's just what I told him, and of course you've only my word that it's true. And all I can say about him is pretty much the same thing. I know his Mackay people out at home, or some of them anyhow, and better folk don't breathe. And we've talked lots since we left King's Cross, and nothing he has said has contradicted anything I know."

"And I may just add," put in the other, "that both our folks came originally from this part of the world, as you can tell by our names, and we are both on leave and going to look up some of the old people. There's a cousin of my father, an old minister up in Sutherlandshire. And he's got far-out relations there too, I understand."

"That's right." The fair man nodded. "They are farming folk of some kind."

The sailor took up the tale next. "My name's Matthews," said he, "and I'm going up to join a ship at Scapa. I'd tell you her name, only it's against the regulations; and in fact, looking to the present situation and seeing that *someone* is under suspicion, I can't break through them on this occasion. I've no pals to bear me out, but that's my sworn statement—for what it's worth."

"I'm in the same boat," said the guardsman. "I can only say that my name's Hillary, and that I'm in the Grenadier Guards. I'm going up to Scapa too, to put in a week's leave in my cousin's ship, but for the same reasons I can't very well even mention her name."

The civilian spoke last. "My name's Walters," said he, "and as I mentioned before, I'm an official of the board of agriculture for Scotland traveling on official business. Like the last two gentlemen who spoke, I am without witnesses to my identity."

Again there was a pause, and again it was broken by the tall Australian.

"Well," he said, "here we are all together, and if one of us *is* a spy, well, he can't do much spying just for the moment!"

"Yes, I quite see what you mean," agreed the civilian. "I suppose it really wouldn't do to part company till we make sure."

"He didn't quite say that!" exclaimed the sailor. "How could we manage it, all going to different places?"

"Oh, I only thought that was the suggestion," said Mr. Walters hurriedly.

"It's the only thing to be done," said Captain Hillary abruptly.

"Precisely," agreed the tall Australian. "The only difficulty is, how are we to arrange it?"

"Where do you get out?" asked the guardsman.

"Place called Lairg." The tall Australian turned to his companion and added, "You meant to stop not far off there, didn't you?"

"One station beyond," said the fair man, "but getting out at Lairg would make no odds. I can manage that."

"As I was saying, I'm bound for Scapa," said Matthews, "but I can't ask you chaps to go on all that way, and if they don't like my turning up a day late, well, they'll just have to lump it! It's a good enough excuse, I reckon. I'll stop at Lairg too."

"So will I," said the guardsman briefly.

There was a moment's pause while they all looked at Walters.

"Oh, I think I can manage to go on to Lairg," he said after an instant's reflection. "But what do you propose to do when we get there?"

"Well," said Mackay, the tall man, "I suppose we'd better wire the situation to Inverness or somewhere, and just wait at Lairg for instructions."

"That's it," said Matthews, and Hillary nodded approval.

The civilian also nodded, but more thoughtfully, and almost—it seemed—a trifle absently, and he said nothing. The other Australian seemed satisfied also, and now that the arrangement was made, silence fell upon the carriage.

It had been a day of heavy clouds with a gusty wind, and the short afternoon merged early into evening; while, in the spell of absolute silence, the gusts seemed to have risen into squalls, and filled the carriage with constant little sounds. Lieutenant Matthews sucked at his pipe, the two Australians seemed immersed in illustrated papers, Mr. Walters continued to glance through his official correspondence, and the guardsman smoked a cigarette and stared out of the window. None of the five so much as looked at one another.

Suddenly Mr. Walters looked up from his papers and exclaimed, "I am very sorry, gentlemen, to seem to back out of what we have arranged, but I have just realized that my official duties really won't permit of my going through to Lairg tonight. I am afraid I must get out at Tain. I can give you, however, every assurance that no suspicion can possibly attach to me. As I told you, I am a government official, and surely that should be a pretty good guarantee."

He looked towards the Australians as he spoke, and then, a little anxiously one would think, at the R.N.R. lieutenant. These three exchanged glances, and all seemed to hesitate for a moment. The tall Australian spoke first.

"Well," he said, "if you are really traveling on government business, Mr. Walters—and mind you I don't doubt it!—I think that perhaps we might make an exception and raise no objection under the circumstances."

"If the gentleman gives us his word, I'd be quite willing to agree with you," said Matthews.

Sutherland, the fair Australian, nodded, and added, "I'd feel quite satisfied to risk it."

"Thank you, gentlemen, thank you very much," said the civilian gratefully, and turned towards Hillary.

The guardsman shook his head suddenly and firmly.

"I'm very sorry," he said shortly, "and please don't think I suggest any suspicion, but we've made this arrangement, and I'm afraid I shall have to call the guard at once if any one leaves the train before Lairg—just as I should expect you to do if I tried to leave."

For a moment there was an awkward pause, and then Matthews began, "This seems a bit hard on the gentleman if he has really got business. . . ."

Mr. Walters interrupted hastily, "Not a bit; not at all; I quite see Captain Hillary's point. It will be a little awkward for me, but rather than raise any difficulty I shall certainly go on with you to Lairg—certainly."

Matthews seemed about to speak again, but the tall Australian cut in quickly, "Well, that's settled then. I apologize for my share in putting you about."

"And I apologize too," put in Hillary, "but I really think you must see our position yourself."

"Quite, quite, I see it perfectly," said the government official. "Don't trouble to apologize."

The spell of silence that followed was even more strained than the last. At one station the lamps were lit and the blinds drawn down, and just after starting again Mr. Walters made the first remark. "Our next stop is Bonar Bridge," said he. "As that is the only place where one can

get refreshments, and as I have already passed my intended
destination, I think we might all, perhaps, arrange to leave
the carriage for a few minutes, and then any of us who want
it could get a cup of tea. We would, of course, all keep
within sight of one another."

He looked at Hillary as he spoke, and the guardsman at
once nodded a brief assent. "I am quite agreeable to that,"
said he.

"And I, and I," added the others.

It was getting pretty dark when the doors were opened all
down the train, and a crowd in blue and khaki poured
across the platform to the refreshment room. The more dignified demeanor demanded of an officer handicapped the
five in this race, and for two or three minutes they were
passing slowly through the back of the crowd, waiting their
turn. The grenadier was a little apart from the other three
officers, and the civilian was pushing close at his shoulder.
For one single instant Hillary seemed to start, and it looked
as though he were going to turn his head and then re-
frained. He stood quite still, however, with all expression
vanished from his face, and then in a minute slipped forward between two pairs of shoulders to the buffet.

The four officers each returned to the carriage carrying
a cup of tea and took their seats. On the platform the crowd
was breaking up and scattering back to the train, and the
guard was shouting something and waving a lantern.

"Hullo!" exclaimed Lieutenant Matthews. "The board
of agriculture chap hasn't turned up!"

"Is he going to give us the slip after all?" cried Sutherland, and there was more than a trace of excitement as he
gazed through the window.

"Oh, surely not!" murmured Hillary, and yet there was
anxiety in his eye.

This time the tall Australian said nothing, but his brow
was knitted, and in his eye wonder was manifest, and also a

trace of excitement held on the curb. And then he spoke in rather a curious voice. "Ah, here he is!" he said.

The civilian apologized for his delay as he rejoined the four officers. "I'm afraid you must have thought I was going to back out," said he, "but the fact is I thought I was never going to get my cup of tea!"

"That's all right!" said Mackay, quite cheerfully again. "We're used to getting our nerves rattled!"

"Part of our business!" laughed Matthews.

The tension seemed a little relieved now. The Australians, Lieutenant Matthews, and the government official all began to talk in a desultory fashion, and yet with some air of friendliness and less restraint. The guardsman alone kept silent, and picking up a paper studied it apparently with great attention, for it was noticeable that he only turned over a page once in every ten minutes or so.

Outside, over the empty moor and somber seas of pines, the darkness deepened till night had fallen quite. At one station and then another the train stopped and waited interminably. They were off again and had run for only a few minutes when once more the carriage began to jolt and slacken speed, and then in a moment ceased to move at all. On the instant the tall Australian sprang to his feet and sent the blind flying up and the window down. He looked for a second into the night, and then with a note of agitation cried, "There's some sort of accident! Tumble out quick, you chaps!"

As he spoke his hand was on the door handle, but before he could even turn it, the voice of the civilian rang out sharp and loud, very differently from the voice they had heard before. "Drop that handle or I fire! Hands up, all of you!" And then to Hillary he cried, "Knock now! Loud as you can!"

The tall Australian stood looking down the barrel of Mr. Walters' revolver, his muscles paralyzed, his face a study in mixed emotions. Sutherland and Matthews each made a movement, and on the instant the revolver made a triangular sweep across the three of them. And meanwhile the guardsman was hammering on the partition. All this happened within the space of some five or ten seconds, and then the door was flung open from the outside and a square-shouldered man in plain clothes mounted into the carriage. Behind him was another in plain clothes, and behind him again three or four figures in khaki.

"Arrest these three men!" commanded the late representative of the board of agriculture.

The tall Australian found his voice at last. "What's all this about?" he demanded coolly enough. "What do you take us for?"

"Spies," said the detective quietly.

"Come on; game's up, out with your hands," said the plain-clothes man stolidly.

The handcuffs clinked on the wrists first of the tall man and then of the fair man and then of the R.N.R. lieutenant. A couple of minutes later the civilian and Captain Hillary were alone in the carriage.

"I still can't take it all in," said Hillary. "When you whispered in my ear at the buffet that you were a detective and told me to knock on the partition when you gave me the tip, you dashed near flattened me out on the spot! I had honestly thought that either you were the spy, or that there was some mistake and nobody was!"

The detective smiled. "I had only made up my own mind a few minutes before that."

"What! Didn't you know who were the spies all the time?"

"Not for certain. I don't mind telling you now, Captain Hillary, that we had information which led us to suspect very strongly that a spy, or possibly more than one spy, was probably going to try to get through on this train. Also we suspected that the uniform of a colonial officer would probably be the disguise. But that was all I had to start on, and I didn't know my man by sight, or whether there would be more than one, or even whether there would be anybody on this train at all."

"Then how did you get on their track?"

"Well, luckily there was a very small selection of overseas officers starting from King's Cross, and only these two went north of Inverness. I'd fastened on to that tall chap from the beginning simply by instinct and experience, but I wasn't a bit sure that the other fellow mightn't have been the genuine article. As for the naval lieutenant, he was a complete surprise package. He took me in fairly for a long while. In fact, if they hadn't been fools enough to travel all three in the same carriage, he'd have got through to Lairg or Cromarty, or wherever he was going, safe enough."

"He said he was going to Scapa."

The detective shook his head. "He might have been, but I don't quite see how he'd have got into Scapa and out again without being spotted. Lairg's the centre for striking off for the northwest corner of Scotland. That's more likely, or else Cromarty. However, he won't get to either place now."

"Then when did you know that all three were spies?"

"I'd been noticing a few little things—looks passed between them and so on; but what settled it was when I pretended I wanted to get out at Tain and all three of them agreed to it. And that was when you cleared your own character, Captain Hillary!"

Hillary laughed. "Lucky for me I was rude to you!"

"And unlucky for them they didn't take the same line. They might have kept me wondering a bit longer. But they all three jumped a little too quickly at the chance of being left with only one man to deal with." The detective's face lit up with a smile of reminiscent admiration. "I must say, though, that tall fellow was a clever chap! When I let him in for that arrangement of all keeping together, he played the innocent manly sort of game uncommonly well!"

"He took me in completely," said Hillary, "but then, of course, I'm an innocent fathead in these matters." He paused and looked across at the other. "By Jove, now one comes to think of it, that was a fatheaded sort of thing one of those fellows did—carrying about that envelope with a German address on it! What on earth was he doing with it?"

The detective seemed to look at him rather oddly. "It almost seemed as though it had been dropped just to provide an excuse for keeping the company from separating," he suggested drily.

The young officer laughed. "Great idea, bringing an envelope from Germany for that purpose!"

"That envelope was addressed in this carriage," said the detective gravely.

Hillary stared at him. "What! But it was torn and dirty! Besides, how. . . ."

"It was torn by the fatheaded chap who addressed it. He tore it because it hadn't a German stamp and postmark on it, and the whole envelope would have given the show away. As for when he did the tearing, it was when the old general got out and he jumped out too. And he dirtied it by putting the piece he meant to drop under his foot while he was standing on the platform."

"By Jove!" murmured Hillary, and then suddenly burst into a roar of laughter. "How those three must have wondered which of his pals had done such a silly thing!"

A MAN'S FOES

PEARL S. BUCK

Martin Liu was bewildered as he stepped out of the train at the railroad station in Peking. Nothing was changed, it was exactly as he remembered it for the seven years he had been abroad. But he had so long looked forward to this moment of homecoming that now it was come it was unreal.

He stood, looking about him, and at that instant saw Wang Ting, his father's chief secretary, and his own sister Siu-li. They were looking in the crowd for him and he now saw them first. He shouted and Siu-li saw him and waved a gay pink handkerchief. She came toward him eagerly; the elderly secretary followed her. Martin had not seen this twin sister of his all these years. He had thought of her much and though he had seen many pictures of her he was not quite prepared for this extremely pretty and poised young woman who put out her hand.

"Elder brother!" she cried in a soft voice. He was older than she by two hours.

"Is this you, Siu-li?" he inquired, unbelieving.

"It is no other, certainly," she replied, smiling. "But here's Wang Ting, too."

Wang Ting came bowing and Martin bowed. He remembered with affection this man who had stood as his father's deputy as long as he could remember. That Wang Ting was here now meant that his father was not. He was disappointed, though he had known his father might not come to meet him. Still, after seven years, and he an only son. . . .

"Is father well?" he asked Siu-li.

He noticed the smallest of hesitations before she answered.

"Yes, he is well. Today it happens he has important business or he would have come."

Wang Ting cleared his throat. "Your father sent every message of welcome by me," he said solemnly. "And he says he hopes you will not delay. There are guests invited for a feast at seven, and it is now nearly half past five. You will want to rest and he will want a few moments at least with you alone."

Wang Ting stepped back, having done his duty.

"Thank you," Martin said courteously.

"Let's go home quickly," Siu-li said with an unexpected petulance. "Wang Ting, you see to his bags and trunks. We will go on."

Wang Ting bowed and took the checks that Martin handed to him. A few minutes later the brother and sister were sitting side by side in their father's car.

They said nothing for a short while. Each was shy of the other, now that they were alone. Though they were fully aware of their relation, still it remained true that they were a young man and a young woman, strange to each other. Then Martin forgot himself.

"I don't remember this road," he remarked. "I thought we used to go to the right."

"We always did until the Japanese came," Siu-li said. "Now we go this way so as to avoid their chief barracks."

"I see," Martin said. He knew that the Japanese had full possession of Peking. Even if his father and sister had not written him of it he would have known it from reading the newspapers in New York, where he had been a student. At first he had expected every letter to tell him that his family had moved away, but as time went on and this did not happen he began to believe that things had not changed so much as he had feared they would. Evidently it was still possible for proud Chinese like his father to live under a Japanese flag, although of course it would be only temporary. It was unthinkable that the Japanese would continue to rule in China. That was why he had come back to China with only a master's degree. His father had urged, indeed, had commanded him to remain abroad for two more years at least and if possible longer in order to get practical experience in his chosen field of metallurgy.

"China needs men of the highest training," his father had written.

But Martin, reading in the American newspapers about the way Japanese soldiers were behaving in his country, could not keep his blood calm enough to sit studying.

"I must come back and do what I can now against the enemy," he wrote his father. And without waiting for reply he had drawn his next term's expense money out of the bank and bought a ticket for China. He had expected questions and even trouble at the port; but when he had given his father's name there had been no trouble and the questions had ceased.

"Do the Japanese annoy you on the street?" he asked his sister now.

Again there was that faint but unmistakable hesitation in her answer. Then she said: "Sometimes—no, not if they know who I am." Her face shadowed. "But I hate them!" she said in a low voice. "I want to avoid them!"

"Of course," he agreed. He was glad to avoid them, too, and he said nothing when the chauffeur drove slowly through small winding alleys instead of the wide main streets of the city.

When the car drew up finally before the gate of his father's home, his throat tightened. He was really home at last!

"It looks just the same," he said, gazing at it.

It was just the same, the wide wooden gates painted vermillion red and set in the thick brick wall and over the wall the old twin pomegranate trees of the entrance court.

"How the trees have grown!" he said.

"Seven years," Siu-li said smiling. "I've grown, too, and so have you."

"Yes," he said.

Then he saw something was changed after all. Instead of the one watchman he had been used to see at his father's gate, he now saw two soldiers, uniformed, their bayonets fixed. They presented arms smartly as he stepped from the car and he was embarrassed.

"What's this?" he whispered to Siu-li when he had returned their salute.

"Father has to have a bodyguard just now," she said in a voice whose quality confounded him. It was angry with scorn.

But she led the way quickly into the gate and there was no time for questions. The first courtyard was full of eager servants, waiting to welcome home the son of the house.

Firecrackers exploded and banners waved. He had to speak to all the old ones and to acknowledge the bows of the new. Even his old wet nurse was there, come in from the country for this day. His mother had died at the birth of the twins, and while Siu-li had her own nurse, Ling Ma had fed Martin and taken care of him when he was too big to suckle. Everyone had expected his father to take another wife but he had never done so.

"But where is father?" he asked his sister when it was over at last.

"He seems not to have come home yet," she replied. She hesitated, then went on. "Why don't you go to your room and change your things? By then surely he will be back."

"I will," he replied.

They stood a moment, he feeling that she was about to speak of something. But she did not. She touched his hand merely.

"It is very good to have you home again," she said and left him.

His own room was not changed at all. Its wide paper-latticed window looked out into his own small courtyard. The bamboos, the pine, were the same. Bamboos attained their growth in a single year and seven years were nothing to the pine, already two centuries old.

Japan and China, he thought, and was pleased with his comparison.

The door opened and Ling Ma came, her face all loving solicitude.

"Now, heart of my flesh, you are not to touch anything. I will unpack your garments and fold them away."

"Foreign suits must be hung, not folded, Ling Ma," he said.

"Then show me one and I will do the others," she said. "You must rest yourself, you must eat and sleep and play after all these years of study. You are too thin." She came close and searched his face. "You didn't take a foreign wife!"

Martin laughed at her. "No, no wife!"

She nodded her satisfaction. "Then we must see to it. I will talk with your father myself."

Martin sat down in his foreign easy chair. "I haven't seen my father yet," he said.

"Oh, he's busy—very busy," Ling Ma said. She had her face deep in one of his trunks. He could only see her stout back.

"I never knew my father to be busy," he remarked. He could say things to Ling Ma that he could say to no one else.

"He's very busy now," Ling Ma's voice came out of the trunk.

A sudden thought struck him. He put it away and then returned to it. After all, it was only Ling Ma.

"He's not getting married again, is he?" The thought was repulsive, but his father was only fifty years old and it was possible.

"Don't ask me!" Ling Ma's voice was suddenly snappish. She came out of the trunk and her face was very red from bending so long. "Don't ask me anything, Young Master! I don't know anything. If anybody asks me anything about this house, I don't know. I live in the country now with my son, and I only came back to welcome you home, heart of my body."

He was used to outbursts from Ling Ma, for she was a woman of impetuous temper. Now he hardly knew whether there was truth in his suspicion or whether she was angry because she had been treated in some way she considered unfair. Ling Ma had quarreled often over his father's decrees during his childhood, and it might be her old jealousy against authority over the child in her care.

"Did my father treat you unjustly?" he inquired.

She laughed loudly. "Me, little heart? No, I left this house of my own accord. He even invited me to stay and await your coming. But no, I would not. No, it was nothing he did to *me!*"

Ling Ma pursed her lips and looked solemn. He was about to put another question to her. Then he decided against it. He did not wish to resume with Ling Ma the old affectionate childish relationship that gave her power over him. He was a man, now. So he said a little coldly, "That is well, for if he had not given you your due, I should have felt I ought to make amends."

She felt the difference in him and gave way to it at once. "From you I expect only what is good," she said, and then spoke no more, but crept about with her silent solid tread, putting his things right. Then she went away and he was alone.

The house was very still. He had not in years heard such stillness. New York was full of noise, and in its own way, so was the ocean. But this was the stillness of centuries. He felt it around him a protection of strength. What could the enemy do against a great, silent old country?

"They are like swallows attacking a snow capped mountain," he thought proudly.

At that moment to his astonishment the door opened abruptly, and his father came in. "Father!" he cried with joy.

"My son," his father replied. He came forward and seized Martin's two hands and held them closely and gazed into his face.

And Martin, receiving that earnest, questioning gaze, felt suddenly shy. Why had his father done so strange a thing as to come to him in his own room? It was not like the austere man he remembered so to step aside from custom. He had been prepared to go to his father when summoned, to stand while his father sat, to answer when he was questioned. But instead here his father was, an eager, even importunate look upon his aging face. He had aged very much. Martin drew back. Instantly his father loosed his hands and the look disappeared.

"Are you well?" he inquired.

"Quite well," Martin replied. He hurried on, anxious for talk. "I hope you are not angry that I disobeyed you, my father. I felt I must come home now—for two reasons. The first is that I want to be of what use I can against the enemy. The second is that I was honestly ashamed to be living abroad in ease and at study as though my country were not suffering."

His father stood looking at him. "I am not angry," he said. "It would be of little use if I were. This generation does what it pleases."

"No, Father, don't speak so," Martin cried. "It makes me feel you are angry!"

His father shook his head. "No, only certain of your misunderstanding," he said in a low voice.

"Father, how can you say that?" Martin demanded. "I am your son!"

But his father only gave him a melancholy smile. "We will see," he said gently. "Meanwhile, it is time for your guests." He glanced at his son's clothing. "What are you wearing?" he inquired.

"What do you wish?" Martin asked, surprised. He had imagined a dinner of old friends, informal and gay, and he had thought with pleasure of a soft silk robe, easy and cool, which he had not been able to wear for a long time.

"Wear your formal foreign evening clothes," his father said. "And what badges have you? Put on the gold key they gave you, and any other thing you have."

He met his son's stare of astonishment. "I want to be proud of you before my—my friends," he said, and then looked at his watch. "It's late," he muttered and hurried away.

In his room alone Martin dressed himself carefully in his best, stiff shirt, silk vest, tailed coat. He had not worn them since the formal college banquet of his graduation day. He had thought then that he would never wear them again, certainly not in his father's home. More mystified than ever, he put on his Phi Beta Kappa key, and his gold signet ring, and his diamond-studded fraternity pins, one Greek letter and the other the honor society of his profession.

"I have nothing more," he thought. Then he remembered a small pin Siu-li had sent him once in play. It had been attached to the first page of a letter. It was made of silver and enameled in the design of the Chinese flag. Half in fun he took it from the box with his cuff links and pinned it to his lapel.

"Why not?" he thought. "I'm a good Chinese and I'll let the world know it."

He went out of his room, whistling an American tune under his breath. There was no one about, and he sauntered in the direction of the main hall. Then he heard voices and he hurried his steps slightly. It was half an hour beyond seven but he had not expected anyone before eight. If he knew his China no one came on time to a dinner. The noise now was that of many voices. It sounded as though everyone had come.

He drew aside the red satin curtain hanging in the door and looked. The room was large, but there were many there, between thirty and forty, his eye guessed. And then he saw something else. He could not believe it, but it was true. Three fourths of the guests were Japanese! Then his father saw him.

"Come in, my son," he said.

There was nothing for him to do except to obey.

• • •

"You should have warned me," he said to Siu-li.

He had come straight to her room after the interminable dinner was over.

"What do I know to tell you?" she retorted.

The years they had been parted were vanished. His anger and dismay had demanded frankness between them, and she had expected him. When he went to her court the light was shining like moonbeams through the opaqueness of the rice-paper lattice, and he saw the shadow of her head bent over a book.

"You should have told me what people are saying," he replied.

"What are people saying except what they, too, do not know?" she retorted again.

"At least you should have told me that my father has Japanese friends," he said.

"But he has always had friends among foreigners in Peking," she said stubbornly. "And some have always been Japanese. The Baron Muraki has been his lifelong friend and you know it."

Yes, he knew it. When he was a little boy Baron Muraki, even then a kindly, aging man, used to bring him miniature rickshas and animals and tiny fish of gold-washed silver. Nevertheless he said, "No one can have Japanese friends now."

"I have told Father that, too," Siu-li said quietly.

"What did he say?" Martin demanded.

"That he had seen too many wars to allow them to change his friendships," she replied.

They looked at each other with the tragic and absolute despair of the young.

"It is such men who will lose our country for us," Martin cried, "and I shall tell him so!"

"You will tell Father that?" she cried.

"I'm not afraid of him, anymore, not after tonight," he

told her. "If you could have seen him, Siu-li, bowing to those strutting little men, the gold on their uniforms like scabs! And calling them carefully by their titles, General This and General That! And pressing the best of everything on them and watching them grow drunk as though they were doing him a favor. I could scarcely swallow, though I've been thinking for years of eating shark's fins again and spit-roasted duck!" His young face gloomed at her, and she cried, "Ah, it is hateful, but how can you say anything to Father?"

"I can," he retorted. "These are not the times of Confucius."

He strode away on this strength to his father's court. But it was now very late. The rooms were dark around the large silent court where his father lived so much alone. He hesitated and knew he dared not knock in spite of his angry courage.

"I will wait until tomorrow," he thought, and tiptoed away. It would be all the better to wait, he told himself, back in his own room. He could speak calmly and reasonably in the morning. After all, his father was an old man and it was possible that he did not know what he was doing. It was hard to imagine that the keen eyes of his father did not see all that went on before them, but the time must come for him to fail as for all men. He sighed, tried to sleep, and could not until it was nearly dawn. Then he slept long and extravagantly, and it was noon when he was awakened by Wang Ting, standing by his bed.

"Your father commands your presence," Wang Ting said.

And out of old habit Martin leaped to his feet.

What he must remember, he told himself an hour later, in his father's study, was that old bonds were broken between a man and his son. What the revolution had begun this war had finished. Everywhere young men and women were telling their parents that their country must come first. "Patriotism is higher than filial duty," they were telling old people who felt themselves deserted.

He struggled against the bonds still strong between himself and this tall, slender, silk-robed man. It was hard to believe so dignified a gentleman had been the one he had watched last night. When Martin thought of this his will hardened. His father had been that man, nevertheless.

"Sit down, my son," his father told him.

He sat down, not cornerwise as he had been taught to sit in an elder's presence but as one man sits in the presence of another. If his father noticed this, he made no sign of it.

"There are many things between us for talk," his father said. "And yesterday I was busy."

"Your time is no longer your own," Martin said boldly.

His father threw him a sharp look. "It is true I am busy," he said smoothly. Something crept over his face like a veil, leaving it expressionless. Against it Martin suddenly rebelled. The last seven years had been spent among frank and impulsive foreigners, and he would not return to careful speech.

"I shall speak plainly," he told his father. "I was surprised to see our enemies in this house."

"Baron Muraki—" his father began.

But Martin interrupted him. "The baron was only one of nearly a score."

The look on his father's face grew closer.

"Do you accuse me?" he asked gently.

"I do," Martin said. His eyes were steady upon his father's face. But his father's eyes did not turn either.

"Does it occur to you that I may have my reasons?" he asked.

"There can be no reason, now," Martin declared. Small things he had forgotten were coming back to him. In New York a Chinese classmate had suddenly declined further friendship with him. When Martin pressed him one day with an invitation the young man had said curtly, before he turned away, "My father does not know your father."

It had seemed foolish then to give as cause against friendship that a Chinese merchant in New York had not known a Chinese gentleman in Peking.

"That can scarcely be expected," Martin had said haughtily and thereafter had ignored the man. Now he understood.

And Ling Ma last night—now he understood her hints.

"Do you know, Father, what people are saying about you?" he demanded.

"I have never known what they say, because I have not cared," his father said calmly.

"You must care now; they are saying you are a friend of the Japanese." He watched his father's face. It did not change.

"I have always had my friends among the Japanese," he said.

"They are saying you are a traitor," Martin rose to his feet.

His father's face did not quiver. "Do you believe them?" he asked.

Martin saw curiosity in his look, nothing else. He was suddenly full of angry certainty. Nobody, he thought, had ever known his father well. He had come and gone in this house, a cold and dignified figure whom they had feared.

"I do not know what to believe," he said.

There was a long pause, then his father spoke, "You will believe what you want to believe," he said. "That is the habit of the young."

"And is that all you will say?" Martin demanded.

"That is all," his father replied.

They were both very angry, and Martin was the more angry because he was less able to control himself than his father.

"I cannot stay in a house where enemies are accepted as friends," he said proudly.

"Do you mean my house?" his father inquired.

His blandness drove Martin to his last step.

"Yes," he said.

He rushed from the room. He had exiled himself the day after he had come home. Where now could he go? Siu-li must know. She must help him. He went to find her. She was in her courtyard sprinkling small gray orchids in the rocks, her fingers dipping in and out of a pewter bowl she held.

"I have told Father I cannot stay," he said to her.

She turned, and the bowl dropped from her hand.

"You have quarreled with him?"

"Yes—forever," he said. "And you must come too, Siu-li. Only traitors can live in this house. You must come!" he insisted when he saw her face. "I can't leave you if Japanese men are to be allowed to come and go here. But where shall we go?"

She stooped and picked up the bowl.

"I have it already long planned," she said softly. She glanced about the small courtyard. "Twice, I didn't know whether I could stay. There is an old general—did you see him last night? The one with the small white mustache?"

"Yes," he said, and his gorge rose.

"Well, that one—once he saw me, and he asked for me to be brought in." Disgust was dark upon her face.

"Did Father send for you?" Martin cried.

"Yes. I didn't know why, or I would not have gone. When I entered the main hall the old general was there."

"But—but—what did Father say?" Martin was bewildered. This was not like his father.

"He said he thought modern young women could take care of themselves," Siu-li said. A slight pink rose in her cheeks and she went on. "The truth is we had quarreled the

day before, Father and I. He did not want me to go to a
dance at the Grand Hotel. I wanted to go and I went. So
perhaps he was punishing me."

"It was not suitable publishment," Martin cried.

They stood full of mutual anger.

"We must go," he repeated.

"It could be to the Northwest," she said. "I have a friend
who knows the way. A girl, a soldier."

"Communist?" he asked.

"Guerrilla," she amended.

"Where?"

"I can send her a message for tonight. She comes and
goes," Siu-li replied. "She is here now in the city. When
she goes back we can go with her. She has ways."

He thought hard for a moment. Into the Northwest! It
was the birthplace of bandits and war lords in the old days,
the stronghold of Communists in the new. He had seen men
from the Northwest, camel drivers and traveling merchants,
soldiers and wandering priests. They spoke with a burr
upon their tongues that was foreign to him, and they were
more foreign to him than the Americans among whom he
had lived. And he was loath to leave this home to which he
had looked with longing all his years away from it. Life in
Peking was easy and beautiful.

But not now, he thought, and aloud he said, "It may as
well be there as anywhere."

Siu-li wavered one moment before she spoke, but only
one.

"I also," she said firmly. She looked down and saw the
pewter bowl in her hand and in a gesture of recklessness she
lifted it up and threw it over the wall.

He was forever after to divide his life into two parts, that
before he knew Meng-an, and all that which came to him
afterwards. The question which he put to himself often was

why he did not at once see her for what she was. But he did not. On the day on which he and Siu-li left their home with her, he saw his sister's friend as a small inconspicuous creature, so like a young boy in her peasant garb that it took faith to believe her a girl. He had seen plenty of girls in America, athletic girls, boyish girls, strong-bodied and clear-eyed girls. But one always knew they were girls. Meng-an was without sex, he thought, looking at her again and again, even that first day.

Though why did I look at her so often? he inquired of memory.

She was not beautiful. An earnest face, an unchanging mouth with small full lips, eyes very black and white, short shining black hair, skin as brown as a peasant's and a slim breastless body, carried like the soldier she was, though she wore no uniform now. He said for days of hard journeying, always westward, that there was no allure in this little creature. She seldom talked and when she did she seemed purposely brusque and plain. But though she was small, she was merciless in her strength. She could walk endlessly and ride anything of a beast. Once she leaped astride a farmer's ox as it pulled a wooden cart. And she had refused the motor car Siu-li had suggested bringing the day they started.

"Why trouble ourselves with a machine we can use only for a few miles?" she said scornfully.

He did not at that moment realize all that her words meant. They had left home quite openly one clear summer's day. Each carried a knapsack and no more. Their father never rose until noon, and Wang Ting meeting them at the gate smiled and bowed and said, as he hurried on, "You have a lucky day for your holiday."

They had looked at each other and smiled behind his back.

"A long holiday," Martin had said.

They had not walked more than a half a day before Siu-li

was exhausted. The sun grew hot. Meng-an, springing along, her cloth shoes silent in the dust, was merciful.

"You will be able to walk more tomorrow," she said.

She kept watching for a vehicle and in a little while she stopped a farmer returning from market with his wheelbarrow empty and asked for a ride. He was willing enough, but when Meng-an bade Siu-li seat herself he was less willing.

"I thought it was to be you, girl soldier," he complained.

"It is the same, she is my friend," Meng-an replied calmly, and so the farmer pushed Siu-li as far as he was going.

"Why was he willing for you?" Martin inquired, curious to know this small creature's power.

"He knows we work for them," Meng-an answered vaguely. "And I pass here often."

Everywhere it was the same. With an assurance that might have been impudent in another, Meng-an asked and was given. Village bakers gave her bread, at tea shops she was given a pot of tea, and anywhere a small traveling restaurant keeper stirred up a bowl of noodles and vegetable oil and shook his head when she held out the cash.

"We all work for the country," he would say, a little pompously.

They depended on Meng-an for everything and the more as they came into the Northwest where she knew all and they knew nothing. By now Siu-li wore man's clothing that she might walk more freely, and Martin wore peasant's garments, and Meng-an wore the ragged boy's clothing that she always put on when she entered land held by the enemy. They walked until noon, ate, slept by the roadside, and walked again until midnight. This they did day after day until it became the habit of their lives. Every other thing they had once done now grew dreamlike in their memories.

"I wonder if Father minds that we are gone?" Siu-li said one day as they rested for a moment.

"He knows why we went," Martin replied.

Meng-an's eyes were upon the bare and distant hills.

"I have not seen my parents for six years," she said suddenly.

"Do you long for them?" Siu-li asked.

"Sometimes," Meng-an said. "Then I remember that if I return to them I return to all the old life—marriage to a man I do not know, a courtyard with the gates locked. And then I get up and go on."

She had never said so much. There was a flicker in her eyes as she spoke but no more. But Martin thought to himself that this small creature had felt things that he did not know.

"Were you early betrothed?" he asked.

She nodded, but did not speak, and he could not for decency ask again.

All these days they had been walking through enemy-held country. Had they been without Meng-an they would have been stopped before this by enemy soldiers. But Meng-an knew how to come and go as a mouse does in a crowded house. Everywhere she was told by someone, a beggar, a farmer, a priest, if there were enemy soldiers near, and then she led them differently, by secret devious ways of her own. Never once did they meet the enemy face to face.

"Though sometimes I do," she told them.

"What then?" Martin asked. He watched her while she answered. Upon that small inscrutable face he was beginning to discern changes, slight to an unseeing eye, but vivid to him. This girl could feel.

"I always pretend to be a fool," she said. "Like this—"

By some trick she threw her lower jaw crooked and crossed her eyes and looked an idiot. She straightened herself again.

"Then they let me pass."

"I should think so," Siu-li said, laughing.

But Martin said nothing. At this moment he was not sure whether a girl should be like this Meng-an. There she sat, on a side of the dusty road where they had stopped for a rest. Her hair was brown with dust, and dust lay in shadows on her face.

"She is not beautiful," he thought, "though brave."

And then that night they passed out of enemy-held country and into their own. He could feel the difference, or thought he could, even in the twilight air. Certainly people were more free in their talk and their laughter at the inn where they lodged, and there was much boasting of how this one and that had crept in and out of the enemy line. But Meng-an was the most changed of all. When they reached the inn she went into one room awhile. A little later she came out for the evening meal. Martin had washed himself and changed his garments. But he was not prepared for what he now saw. A slim young soldier came out of the room Siu-li and Meng-an shared, a soldier in a clean khaki uniform, belted and buttoned and with a small pistol at the waist. It was Meng-an. When she saw him she saluted and gave him the smallest of smiles. It was the first she had ever given him.

"You must go to our general," Meng-an told him. Three days more had brought them to the stronghold of this Chinese army to which she belonged. For three days they had walked among a tranquil people, tilling and working the land as though war were in another world. Night brought them to the camp itself, where he would go to the men's division and Siu-li and Meng-an to the women's. They halted at the gate of the temple compound where guards stood. Once inside they must part. Thus Meng-an had paused to speak.

"I will see him tonight," she went on, "and when I have given him my secret messages from the old city, I will tell him of you. He will be glad, for he needs men like you."

Now Martin did not want to part from her.

"When shall we see each other?" he said boldly.

The flicker in her eyes he could discern but not its meaning. Was it feeling for him or against him? He did not know.

"There are many meetings for us all," she said, and whether it was promise or evasion he still did not know. And she gave him no time to think. She led the way inside the gate and they were parted. He was given food and a bed and by dark he slept as all slept, because light at night meant oil and oil was money, and money must be spent on bullets for the enemy.

At dawn he rose, called by a bugle, and after food Martin was summoned by a young man so carelessly clothed as a soldier that on the upper part of him he wore a farmer's coat.

"Are you the son of Liu Ming Chen?" he inquired abruptly of Martin.

"How do you know my father's name?" Martin asked.

"We all know it," the man replied.

Martin was silenced by fear. Why should all here know the name of his quiet scholar father in Peking except now as a traitor? He said nothing.

"The general calls you," the man said. "Follow me."

Without hesitation Martin followed and found himself in the doorway of the cave house where the general lived at the back of the temple as many did here, among these high barren mountains. But this room was comfortable with furniture and the floor was rock swept clean. The general was not a fat old man but a young, thin-bodied man in faded uniform. No one could have said he was anything more than another, except agile and clever, relentless if he were an enemy.

"One tells me you know metals," he said to Martin without greeting.

That one, Martin knew, was Meng-an. He wondered jealously if she knew this man well and if they were friends. He had missed her already, for when he woke he wondered if today he would see her and how and when.

"It is true," he replied.

The young general looked at him shrewdly.

"You left your father," he said.

"Yes," Martin said. The man knew that!

"Many leave their parents these days," the general said gravely. "Once when I was a child I was sent to a Christian school. In their sacred book I found one day by chance words like this: 'And a man's foes shall be they of his own household.' I who had been taught the doctrine of Wu Wei, I thought, 'How evil are these Christians not to know filial duty!' But the days are come." He paused a second. "I, too, left my parents. We must seek a new foundation for the state, lest we be lost."

The general's accent was not that of a peasant.

"Did you go abroad?" Martin asked.

"Yes. Who told you?" the general replied.

"No one—but where?" Martin asked again.

"To Harvard and to Leipzig," the general said.

"And you are here," Martin said. It was wonder enough.

"I would be nowhere else," the general said. He hesitated a moment, and then went on. "Out of these inner regions will come those who will take back the land."

"But do these people know they are being attacked?" Martin asked. "They are so calm and they work in their fields as they always have."

"By day," the general broke in. "By night they put down their hoes and take their guns. But by what good luck you came I cannot say. We lack iron, and there is ore in these hills. The rocks shine when they are split. Is that iron? If it is, I will set about mining it out. It may be silver, and it is not so quickly useful. Do you see your task?"

"Yes," Martin said. He was looking at the seamed side of the cave as he answered. In the rocks was his task. He must find iron to make bullets for the enemy.

"Have you any message for your father?" the general asked abruptly. "Meng-an will start for Peking tonight."

"She goes back?" Martin cried.

"It is her work—to slip between the enemy armies and find out everything and bring me word."

"She told you of my father," Martin said.

The general nodded.

"No, I have no message for him," Martin said.

The general nodded again. "Then you may go," he told him.

He did not see Meng-an again. When he reached his tent six men were waiting. When they saw him they saluted.

"We are to go with you into the hills," they said.

By some means they had with them the few tools he needed, pickaxes, baskets for rock fragments, materials for mapping, and rolls of bedding.

"At once?" he asked.

"It is so ordered," they replied.

"But I must see someone before I go," he protested.

"We will wait a few minutes," a soldier said, "at your command."

"Let it not be longer, sir," another said. "The general does not like delay."

No, he would not, Martin knew, thinking of that firm young figure. He had turned away and at the door of the women's barracks he asked the girl soldier on guard for Siu-li, and was told to wait.

She came a few moments later and quickly he told her his orders.

"And you?" he asked.

"I am to go into training, merely," she said.

"And Meng-an?" he asked, wanting only to hear of her and knowing very well that he knew more than Siu-li did.

"I have not seen her," Siu-li replied.

He knew he should tell nothing he had been told and yet he wanted some communication with that small creature slipping her lonely way among the enemy. He said in a low voice, too low for the waiting guard to hear, "If you see her today, tell her I said to take care for herself as she goes." And then when he saw the astonishment in Siu-li's eyes he added quickly, "She is more value than you know—to the cause, I mean."

But Siu-li was shrewd with the shrewdness of a woman.

"I was about to ask you now that we are here if you regret coming, but I think I need not," she said.

He laughed sheepishly, feeling himself grow red.

"No, you need not," he agreed. "I am not sorry."

Weeks passed him, and he spent them day upon day in searching the barren hills. They were not barren, he was beginning to discover. Under their sandy tawny surfaces there was rock and in the seams of the rock minerals. He walked up the steep beds of mountain streams, his eyes upon every glint and glitter. The men with him were well chosen, for they were men who belonged to the hills, who had spent their youth washing the streams for silver.

"But is there iron?" he asked them as he asked the hills themselves.

"That we don't know, for we never looked for it when there was silver," they said.

In their fashion they had mined some parts of the hills, and they led him to shallow pits they had dug. There he tapped and examined and tested the fragments he chose. There was silver everywhere, but he could not find iron.

"We may have to make our bullets of silver," he thought grimly.

The strange hills surrounded him, and silence was their atmosphere. There seemed no life in them, and yet sometimes he came upon a monastery built out of sandy rock and seeming in its shape and color so like a cliff that only a gate told the difference. Inside the priests lived, silent so long that they could scarcely speak when he spoke, men whom the mountain winds had dried and beaten upon and bleached until they too were sand colored. And yet every one of them when he told them his task, was eager to help him and to show him certain dark ledges they had seen. Every one of them knew that they had an enemy.

Everywhere they knew. In the night under the endless clear skies and beneath the sharp stars he thought of those who were farmers by day and soldiers by night, and he thought of priests who wanted no peace, and of his sister, who had been so tenderly reared, learning to march long hours and to fire a gun, and most of all and longest he thought of Meng-an making her lonely way in and out among the enemy.

She has the hardest and most dangerous work of us all, he thought. When he thought of this his bitterness against his father heaped itself up with gall. He betrays every one of us, he thought.

The filial piety he had been taught he put from him forever, that ancient teaching which had tied together the generations of his people.

"I am no more his son," he thought. And he thought, "We must build a new country, and every generation must be its own lawmaker."

"There is no iron," he told the general.

"There must be," the general said. "Go back."

The hills were bitterly cold now with autumn. The foolish silver was rich everywhere. But the hills held nothing more. He had stayed a month, and then the cold rain had driven him down from the summit. Then it had seemed he must make report of having found nothing. And he knew, too—the long silent nights and the hot moons had told him —that he longed to see Meng-an. Had she come and gone safely? He must know or thought he must. And so he had come down. He had gone at once to Siu-li. But Siu-li was not there. She had been sent the day before with her regiment to a village to the east to make forays by night against an enemy garrison. He was sick with alarm when he heard it, and then dismayed because she was gone and there was no one he could ask of Meng-an. Everyone went about his business here, and it was no one's business to speak of Meng-an. He had had to go then to the general.

"Go back," the general said now.

And against his look there was no hope of refusal. Besides how could he say, I cannot, until I have seen a certain woman, and how could he even say, I must hear first if Meng-an is safe?

The general saw his hesitation. "We are still at war," he said. "Why do you delay?"

"I do not," Martin said doggedly.

He went back that same day.

He had lived in the hills so long now that when he thought of cities and of people they were words and nothing more. Had he once seen ships and trains and traveled upon them? Even his memories of them were gone. He had for companions these men as dogged as himself and for his strength his own determination that if there was iron in these hills he would find it. And if he had needed a spur to prod him he had it. One day when in an October as cold as winter where he was, he sat on a rock near a summit eating his bread and salt fish, at noon, he saw even there an airplane. It flew well above the mountain top and yet close enough for him to see it. It was an enemy plane! He could see its markings clearly above him as he looked up at it. It sank a little as though it saw him, then rose and sped on. An enemy plane over these far, inner mountains? He swallowed his food quickly and called his men. They were eating fifty feet below him in a shallow valley. He had climbed out of it to see the hills while he ate.

"Come on!" he cried, and when they were come he said, "We must make haste if the enemy has flown as far as this."

They had worked longer after that, and every day they searched the skies. There were no planes for ten days more, and then eleven planes flew over them like wild geese.

That was the day he found iron. He found it early in the morning, low, near the base of the peak upon which he had spent uselessly nearly fifteen days. He had gone too high. The iron was old, and aeons had driven the deposits deep into the bowels of the mountains.

"Have I been looking too high, everywhere?" he asked himself.

He was so excited by this possible thing that he went no higher. He covered half the base of the mountain by noon and in seven places he found signs of iron; whether it was seven different places or all one great rich vein he did not know. But when he sat down at noon, he ate his bread in such excitement that he could scarcely swallow.

Then it was he heard the planes, and looking up he saw their geese-like passage. The sight might only yesterday have filled him with despair. But today he shook his fist at them and with his mouth filled with bread he shouted, "We have our bullets for you!"

Now he could go back with good news. He was even glad that he had found iron in autumn instead of spring. Soon it would be too cold for the enemy planes to fly over the inland, and during the winter months the mines could be planned and made ready. He had long talks about machinery with his men. When he thought of machinery for mines he was troubled. How could they construct and haul and place those great masses? But these men had been miners without such aid. Bamboo and ropes and wooden buckets were their utensils, and Martin listened to them. "A little more than they have had and it will be much," he thought as they went on.

Everywhere through the countryside there were signs of autumn. The harvests were good, and the farmers grew bold to reap them, because few airplanes came now to bomb.

"In the summer we spend half the day in our bomb huts," they told Martin. "Well, it's cool there!" they said, grinning with mischief.

"Well, we have had bandits of many kinds," another said. Wherever he went there was no talk of hardship or surrender, only of how work could be done, whether the enemy came or not.

I wish my father could be here, he thought. If he saw these people, could he still betray them?

The thought of his father was like a sore in his heart. Whatever he did, he thought, it would not be enough to atone for his father. And when he thought of Meng-an he asked himself what right he had, the son of a traitor, to think of her.

In this mood he walked the miles back to the encampment and, without asking of his sister or Meng-an, he went, dusty as he was, to report to the general. In his hand he carried the fragments of rock and he laid them upon the table.

"I have found iron," he said simply, "and plenty of it." The news was enough of itself.

The general took up the rocks as though they were gold.

"Better than gold," he said. Then when he had examined them he looked up at Martin. "When can you go back?" he asked.

"Today, if you bid me," Martin replied steadily.

But the general laughed. "Now you are taught," he said. "It is the answer I wanted. But you shall not go today. We must make our plans."

"There is not much time before winter comes down," Martin said doggedly.

"Not much, but a day or two," the general said, "and that is long enough for everything. I have news for you. Do you remember my little spy?"

"Meng-an?" Her name flew out of Martin's mouth like a bird from a cage.

The general nodded. "How did you know her name?" he asked, surprised.

"She brought my sister and me here," Martin said.

"Do you have a sister?" the general demanded of him. "And if you have, why did you not tell me?"

"There was no need," Martin said.

But the general struck a bell on his table. "She must come here, too," he said. "This news is for both of your father's children."

A soldier appeared.

"Go and fetch—what is her name?"

"Siu-li," Martin said. "Of the Third Regiment."

"Surname Liu, name Siu-li, of the Third Regiment," the general ordered. "And tell Meng-an to come also."

"So!" the soldier cried as he had been taught, and saluting he hurried away.

At the mention of his father Martin was afraid. What would the general call good news except that a traitor had been killed? If this was the news he must warn Siu-li first. They must show no grief. He thought quickly.

"Sir," he asked, "may I speak first with my sister? If something has befallen our father, it will be better to prepare her for it."

"Nothing has befallen him," the general replied. He was

turning the fragments of rocks over in his hands, dreaming of the precious stuff they held.

So there was nothing to do except to wait.

"Sit down," the general said and he sat down. It was very hard to wait. The general was looking at the rock now through a small hand microscope.

Then in a while they heard the light quick tread of feet trained to march, the feet of girl soldiers. The general put down his microscope and looked up. The door curtains opened. Two straight slender girls in uniform stood there. They saluted and stood at attention. Meng-an and Siu-li. Martin smiled at Siu-li and looked at Meng-an. His heart rose on a great wave of pride. These two girls in the old days would have been sheltered, helpless creatures behind a courtyard wall; Siu-li even a few months ago had been in her way useless.

"Is this your sister?" the general asked of Martin, but gazing at Siu-li.

"It is she," Martin said, rising to his feet.

"Be at ease, all of you," the general said. He seemed to have forgotten why he had called Meng-an here. "Be seated," he told Siu-li, without taking his eyes from her face. "I have not seen you before," he said.

Siu-li blushed a little. The uniform, her straight-cut hair, the pistol at her belt, her feet in hard leather shoes, none of these could hide what she was, a soft-eyed girl. Those large soft eyes she now turned upon the young general as full of coquetry as though she wore a silk robe and had jewels in her hair.

"I did not know you wished it," she said demurely.

"But I do," the general said.

Meng-an looked at Martin. In her eyes he saw that flickering—it was laughter, surely. He smiled to answer it. It was pleasant to communicate thus with her over those other two. Then Meng-an coughed a small dry cough, and the general glanced at her and remembered.

"Ah, you also," he said but his voice was very different to her. "Yes, and now repeat what you told me. Who told you that the enemy is about to march southward and how we can surprise that march?"

"Wang Ting," Meng-an replied.

"Wang Ting!" Siu-li cried. "But he's my father's secretary!"

Meng-an did not turn her head. She continued to make report, her eyes upon the general's face. "He is sent by his master. Of himself he knows nothing, but his master is in a position to know much and will be as long as his life is spared by the enemy. If they find out he will die. But until that time, I go to a certain small tea shop and there I can be told."

All this Meng-an said in her even voice as though what she said was nothing.

"If I had known there was also you," the general said to Siu-li as though she were the only one in the room, "I would have told you at once what your father was. He has been for us since the city fell. Why do you think this little spy comes and goes except to bring me news from your father?"

Now Siu-li turned upon Meng-an. "And you did not tell me!"

"How did I know what you thought of your father?" Meng-an retorted. "And I have my orders against talk about him with anyone," she added.

"And you," the general said to Martin, "you I wanted to try, to see if you were fit to be your father's son. When you did not give up until you found the iron we need, I said, 'He is fit.'"

"You knew I doubted my father?" Martin asked slowly.

"Your father begged me in a letter to tell you what he was, when I saw the time was right," the general replied.

They sat, these impetuous two, the modern son and daughter of an old Confucian scholar, and humbled themselves in their knowledge. Then suddenly Siu-li began to weep. She turned to Martin.

"We—we were very unjust!" she whispered.

"Yes," Martin said in a daze, "yes, we were." He thought of his old father in the midst of the comings and goings of the enemy in his house, holding his life as lightly as a toy in his hands, and he cleared his throat. "I wish we could tell him so," he said.

"I will tell him," Meng-an said calmly.

"Don't cry!" the general said suddenly to Siu-li.

She looked at him, her great eyes dewy with tears and very beautiful.

"How can I help it?" she said piteously. "I have been a wicked daughter. I ought to have known my father couldn't —be what we thought he was!"

"I say you are not to weep anymore!" the general shouted. "I cannot bear it," he added in a gentler voice.

And then Martin felt his own eyes caught by someone's gaze, and looked up, and there were Meng-an's eyes, holding his, and this time it was as though their hands clasped. And suddenly his heart inquired, Is there any reason now? and then answered itself, There is no reason.

"Now this is all settled," the general said hastily, "and it is time we went back to our work." His eyes took leave of Siu-li's soft black ones, though unwillingly. "Let us proceed," he said sharply. "Soldiers, attention!"

Martin rose. Siu-li and Meng-an leaped to their feet, saluted, wheeled, and marched out.

The general stared after them and sighed. Then he smiled at Martin.

"You are in love with that little spy of mine," he said.

"How—who—?" Martin stammered.

"Ah, I saw it," the general said calmly. "Well, why not?

Everything must go on the same in wartime. Well, you may have my little spy. Tell her so. But she must go on working. We must all go on working."

"Yes, sir," Martin said. He was dazed with the general's calmness over the most enormous thing in the world. Then even as he looked at the general he saw a strange thing happening. Over that firm stern young face he saw a soft sheepish smile appear that turned the general at once into an ordinary young man such as may be seen any spring day in any country.

"Your sister has very fine eyes," he said abruptly.

"They have been so considered," Martin replied.

The general looked startled. "I suppose so," he said unwillingly. He reflected a moment, still staring at Martin without seeing him.

"Why not?" he demanded after a moment.

"Why not, indeed?" Martin replied. "As you said, sir, even in war everything must go on as usual."

They looked at each other for the last part of a moment longer and suddenly they laughed, and then, sharing this laughter in their youth like a cup of wine between them, they laughed again for pure pleasure.

PHYLLIS R. FENNER was born in Almond, New York, and for thirty-two years was the librarian of the Plandome Road School in Manhasset, New York. In 1955 she retired and made her permanent home in Manchester, Vermont. She holds degrees from Mount Holyoke College and from the Columbia Library School, and has traveled extensively throughout this country, Canada, Mexico, and Europe.

Miss Fenner's work has brought her in touch with library schools throughout the country; she has also done book reviewing, given lectures about children's books, and held story hours for children. In addition, she is widely known for her many distinguished anthologies.